KEATON

Mixology

KRISSY V

Copyright

Dedication

Dad, I miss you!

David Leslie Pyne
19/01/1947-15/09/2017

Sand In Your Shorts

1/2 oz Vodka, 1/2 oz Raspberry Schnapps, 1/2 oz Peach Schnapps, 1/2 oz Midori Melon Liqueur, 1/2 oz Triple Sec, ½ oz Sweet & Sour Mix, 2 oz Cranberry Juice, 2 oz Orange Juice

Now Hunter has found Scarlett, I feel like I've lost my wingman. On one hand, it leaves more women for me. On the other hand, I have to do it all myself because he's not there to hook me up. I guess I always knew one of us would meet someone before the other, but for some reason, I thought it would be me. Hunter never got serious with women. However, Scarlett worked her way into his heart very quickly. She really is amazing and he's a lucky man. She was at Sunday dinner with us recently and she fits into our family so well. It's like she's meant to be there.

Of course, the family had to bring up Dakota fucking Ryan. God, even her name sends me into a panic. I hate her with a passion. She's always in my way of winning the major surfing championship titles and it pisses me off.

I'VE WOKEN up at five this morning and I'm getting ready to head down to Bantham to do dawn patrol. I like to be first on the beach so I can figure out the waves and work out which are the best to ride.

It's still a little dark and I know I'll just be catching the sunrise when I get there.

If you've never watched a sunset or sunrise then you're missing out. It's so beautiful and it never ceases to surprise me when I manage to catch one. Even better is when I'm on my board on the waves when the sun sets or rises.

After parking my car and putting my wetsuit on, I take my board off the roof and make my way down to the shore. It looks like I'm the first one here so I run into the sea, jump on my board, and paddle out past the rolling waves. I take the time to sit and watch the sun rising on the horizon with my back to the beach. Once I can see most of the sun, I turn around and paddle far enough in to shore to be able to jump up onto my board and ride my first wave of the day.

Surfing makes me feel like I'm part of the ocean; weightless as my board cuts across the waves, the air cool around me, hearing the break of the wave as water sprays around me.

I land back at shore, run onto the beach, and stand my board upright while I catch my breath. It's like a drug coursing through my veins. I want more. I can never have enough of the adrenalin rush that surfing gives me.

Hearing someone on the beach, I turn and see Dakota fucking Ryan walking towards me. She is wearing a 'barely there' bikini and, for the first time, I appreciate her fine form.

What the fuck am I thinking? I hate her. But, God, she looks good in that bikini.

"See something you like, arsehole?" she shouts, her voice carrying across the wind.

"Fuck off, Dakota. What are you doing here anyway? You don't normally do Bantham."

"How do you know? You're always late getting here. Can't kick the girls out from the night before, I guess." She turns her back to me and starts to get into her wetsuit.

I can't help myself. I watch as she bends over and steps into the wetsuit then shimmies to pull it up. It's too much for me to handle at this time in the morning.

"Jealous much?" I retort, feeling like a child. "I'm off." I run back down to the shore.

Why does she have to be here? She's ruining my perfectly good morning surfing. Turning up in her sexy bikini, trying to put me off. I know what she's up to. Bitch.

I paddle out and ride the next wave back in. It's exhilarating and I need a breather. Dakota runs past me into the sea and paddles her board out past the crashing waves. I pretend not to watch her, but she's such a graceful surfer. The way she handles the board is a huge turn on. It's just a shame it's her and not some other girl. I'd be trying my hardest to get her to ride me anywhere she wants. But I would never go there with Dakota. Not in a million years. Not if she was the last woman on this earth.

AFTER AN HOUR of pushing my limits, trying to beat Dakota on the waves, I'm exhausted and ready to go home. I walk away from the sea and start to make my way up the beach when I hear, "See you soon, Keaton."

I don't even turn to say goodbye to her, I just walk back to my car and drive away.

It bugs me all the way home. Why do I let her annoy me so much?

When I've had a couple of hours sleep and some coffee, I get dressed and head to Mixology to help Hunter out with the orders. He's already there when I arrive.

"Hey. What's going on today?" I ask.

"We've got the spirit order coming in. We've been wiped out the last couple of weeks. It's a good thing, but the orders are getting bigger every week."

"Any ideas yet what we're going to do to draw more punters in?"

"Nah, not yet. Although, I was thinking…"

"Here we go." I laugh. Hunter has some great ideas, but they usually mean lots of work.

"You know when you're taking time off to compete in the World Championships?"

"Hopefully."

"Well, Ainsley and I were thinking about having a special event that week where the customers can watch the Surfing World Championships live here in the bar."

"That sounds like a great idea."

"Well, you are a sort of celebrity around here, after all."

"Yeah, right."

"You are. I know a lot of women who would come down here and watch just for a glimpse of you in shorts."

"All they have to do is give me the eye on a Friday night and they can see more than my shorts." I laugh.

"So true, so true," Hunter says, laughing too.

The door opens, and Ainsley, Zac, and Skylar barrel in.

I love my family; they're always there for me as I am for each of them. We do lots of things together and we have regular lunches.

"Hey, Keaton. What's up?" Zac shouts as he goes to put the kettle on. He doesn't drink anymore, but I always see him with a cup of coffee in his hand.

"I was down at Bantham this morning. Guess who came and spoiled my day."

Zac laughs. "Dakota?"

"Yeah. Dakota fucking Ryan. She was there in her bikini, trying to put me off."

Ainsley starts laughing. "Really? You think because she was wearing a bikini she was trying to put you off? What about wearing a bikini because she was on a beach? Or maybe because she wanted a swim? It's not all about you, Keaton." She shakes her head and smiles.

"Fuck off," I say as I head over to Zac to grab his coffee from him.

"Do you know what I think, Keaton?" Ainsley asks, following me.

"No, but I know you're going to tell me." I sigh.

"I think you like Dakota."

"Stop right there. No. I fucking don't like her."

"Yes, you do. Your body betrays you when she's nearby, doesn't it? Admit it. You hate that you like her so you push her away."

"Do you know what, Ains? You need to see a shrink, really you do. I do not like Dakota Ryan."

"Whatever." Ainsley laughs as she walks into the office.

Hunter starts laughing too. "Right, come on. We need to do this spirit order and see if we can come up with something to bring the crowds in like when we did singles' week."

We spend the next hour working like Trojans, bringing in the spirit bottles, making sure all the bottles are full and ready to be poured tonight.

After a few hours, we leave to go and change and arrange to meet back at Mixology in an hour. I take the time to chill out back home.

Like Hunter, I live by the sea. I could never be far away

from it. It's in my soul and I would die if I didn't hear the waves crashing against the rocks and the cliffs, and the seagulls shouting in the wind.

After I shower and change into my jeans and Mixology t-shirt, I take a cup of coffee out onto my decking, which leads down to my own private little cove. My place only has two bedrooms, a kitchen-cum-diner-cum-living area, and a bathroom. I don't care; I love it. When we get storm warnings, the view is amazing, but when they get really bad, I have to board the windows up. I had to move out once. Nothing was damaged, thank God, but it was scary. As you can imagine, the insurance is horrendous, but it's worth every penny.

I lose track of time, standing here staring out into the sea with my hands wrapped around my coffee cup. The aroma of the coffee mixed with the saltiness in the air makes me feel at home. I've never brought a woman down here. This is my sanctuary and I don't want to spoil it with women hanging around. I keep that to the bar.

It's soon time to go back to work and I look forward to whatever tonight has in store.

IT'S ALMOST CLOSING time on what has been an extremely busy night. There's a blonde giving me the eye; she keeps smiling at me and she's so cute. I know who is going to keep me warm tonight. She walks over to the bar and leans across it. "Hey, sexy. Can I have a cocktail, please?"

"Sure. What do you want?" I smile at her.

"Sex on the Beach, please."

I laugh. All the girls think it's funny to ask for Sex on the Beach. It's just a glorified vodka and orange, to be honest, but whatever floats their boat.

I start pulling all the ingredients together and can feel her watching me as I pour the vodka into the tall shaker. I pour it out and then add the ice, orange, and grenadine, and then I put the lid on the shaker and start shaking. I put on a show and realise that a lot of people have turned to watch me. I spin the shaker in my hand and channel my inner Tom Cruise in *Cocktail*. Smiling to myself, I open the shaker with a flourish and pour the cocktail for her.

She's looking up at me, smiling, and I know I'm onto a sure thing. Leaning across the bar, I whisper in her ear, "You free later?"

Her eyes are wide open. "Yeah, and I don't live far," she says quietly so I nearly don't hear her.

"Great. Don't go too far now."

"I won't, don't worry about that."

I feel her eyes following me for the next hour while I finish serving and tidy up.

I don't know her name, and I don't care. I need to sink myself into a really hot girl and forget all about that bitch Dakota. I'm mad with myself that I'm even thinking about her. "Come on, babe. Let's get out of here. The others can finish up."

She giggles. When I open my arm for her to step under, she does so gladly. We walk out of Mixology and she guides me to her place. It's small and nothing special, but it doesn't make any difference to me; I don't need to approve of my surroundings. When we walk through the door, I push her against the wall and take her mouth with mine. She moans as she pushes against me. I can tell this is going to be fast and furious. I'm hard in a second.

"God, Keaton. You're huge," she says, grabbing my cock through my jeans.

"It's what I can do with it that will rock your world, babe."

She giggles. "Come on then. Show me you're more than just talk." She takes my hand and guides me to her bedroom. As soon as we step through the door, I push her down on the bed and assault her mouth with mine.

She grabs at me, trying to take my clothes off.

"Slow down. This is not a race. We want to enjoy it," I say, trying to calm her down.

"Sorry, it's just I'm so excited. I've wanted you for ages." She pulls me back down to kiss her.

I can't say it back because I've not noticed her until tonight.

I reach down and take her top over her head and see she isn't wearing a bra; makes my life easier. Leaning down, I take one of her tits into my mouth and suck on it. They're quite small and compact, but still, tits are tits.

Moving down her body, I remove her skirt and kiss her from her belly button down. She's moaning, wriggling, and giggling. Once I get her clothes off, I remove my t-shirt and jeans. I'm commando; I never know when I'm ready to *spring* into action.

I roll her over so she's facing the bed and then kneel on the floor behind her. I move her so her pussy is lined up with my mouth and then I attack her from behind. I nuzzle my nose in between her arse cheeks and then I lick her pussy. Flicking her clit, I feel her twitching beneath me. She is extremely sensitive and I just know she's going to go off like a rocket at any minute and I haven't even put a finger inside her.

I rectify that and put one finger in her and then take it out and put in two. She isn't really tight so I take my spare hand, wrap it around my cock, and start pumping it. I want to make sure I'm good and ready for her. All of a sudden, she starts groaning and gyrating against my face and my fingers. I can feel her walls tighten, not much, but tighten they do, and then she screams my name as she comes around me. Good God, she's a screamer.

I ignore my feelings that I'd rather be somewhere else. I need to get one off now because I'm not leaving without an orgasm.

I move away from her and she groans. "Keaton, where are you going?"

"We need protection." I reach into my trouser pocket and take out a condom. I tear the packet then roll it on my cock in one quick move. "Are you ready for me?"

"Oh, I am so ready for you, Keaton. Fuck me hard."

I don't need to be told again. I stand up and lift her arse so it's higher in the air and then line my cock up and slam into her hard. She screams. Of course she does.

I wait for a minute just to give her chance to adjust and for me to catch my breath. Then it's all systems go and I pump in and out of her. I'm sure I hurt her because I'm going that hard. But I want this over with quickly so I can go home. Maybe tonight was a mistake; I'm not feeling it at all.

I keep pumping and then I lean over her and reach around to her front to feel her clit. I lay my finger over it and start rubbing it to try and get her off quicker.

It works. She starts convulsing around my cock and I wait to follow her, but it doesn't work.

Closing my eyes, I try to conjure up the image of one of the girls I had earlier in the week, but that doesn't work either. When I open my eyes and see her, it makes me think of Dakota. I shake my head. I don't want to think about her right now. That's one way of going limp. I chuckle, but all I can see is Dakota laid in front of me with her sexy bikini and her pussy on show, pushing into me.

I can't help myself, my cock gets harder and I pummel the shit out of blondie. She keeps screaming my name, but

I don't hear her voice, I hear Dakota's screaming my name in the height of passion and that is enough to send me crashing over the edge.

Fuck! That woman will be the death of me. Why the fuck was I thinking of her when I was fucking another woman?

After pulling out and cleaning up, I cut and run, leaving blondie behind. She will probably think I'm a bastard for fucking and running, but I need to clear my head. I hate Dakota Ryan even more for ruining my late night fuck.

Ocean Breeze

1-1/2 oz Raspberry Vodka, 1-1/2oz Coconut Rum, 3oz Cranberry Juice, 1-1/2oz Pineapple Juice

My body is so used to chasing the dawn that I can't actually lie in regardless of what time I go to bed. My interlude with blondie last night made me tired so I crashed out quite quickly. But it wasn't exhausting enough that I need to lay in bed all morning. So, I crawl out of bed, flick the kettle on, and grab my board, climbing down the rocky path from my deck and run into the sea. There aren't many waves here, but at least I know I'm going to be on my own. After two or three times riding the waves, I make my way back up to the house. When I have my coffee in my hand, I sit down and look out to sea. This is where I feel most at home. I do a lot of my thinking here.

I'm early for lunch, but I want to spend some time with them and help Mum cook.

I SPEND a couple of hours with Mum and Dad and then I hear the door open and the first of my siblings come barrelling through the door.

"Hi, I'm home!" Hunter shouts. When he walks into the kitchen, he says, "How's things, Keaton? How was the surf?"

"I didn't go down today. Had too much to do at home."

"Does it have anything to do with that blonde you took home last night?" He smirks.

I pull a face at him for saying it in front of Mum. She knows we like a lot of women, but she doesn't need it pushing in her face.

Hunter shrugs, laughs, and goes into the lounge. I follow him and I'm not surprised to see Scarlett sitting on the couch already. He picks her up and puts her on his lap; there's not much room for everyone to sit. She giggles.

I watch them for a few minutes and wonder what it would be like to be in love like they are. It's all consuming, but so natural. Hunter was the biggest player I knew, apart from me, and within a couple of days, he totally changed and didn't want anyone except Scarlett. I hope I have that kind of love one day. But not today. Today, tomorrow, and the next day, I will be a player. I laugh to myself.

Ainsley comes in next and says hi to everyone before throwing herself on the couch next to Hunter and Scarlett. Scarlett is working with Ainsley and they have become best friends. Talking of best friends, I can't believe Scarlett is best friends with Dakota fucking Ryan. Talk about a small world.

Zac is next and he comes in looking like he's just been to the gym. He's pumped up, and his skin is glistening so he's straight out of the shower and I'm sure he keeps getting bigger and bigger. If he wasn't my brother he would scare me.

"What's up?" he asks as he comes in and sits in one of the armchairs. He looks around. "Where's Sky?"

"He's not here yet," I say.

"I see that!"

Okay, he must have got out of bed the wrong side today.

We hear the front door slam and Skylar walks in. "Hi," he says as he finds a chair to sit in. "What's going on?"

"Nothing that I know about," I say.

"Well let's discuss the next big event we need to have. Mixology is on everyone's lips and we need to keep it that way," Hunter says. "So, what are everyone's ideas?"

"Not sure. We can't do singles' week again for a while," Zac says.

"What's worked well for us in the past?" Skylar asks.

"Everything, to be honest. Whenever we put on events, whether they're planned or impromptu, they always do well. It's about the marketing and the advertisements. That's what really matters. The more time to do that, the better," Ainsley says.

"Yeah. Social media is huge these days and they've moved onto different apps now as well."

"I was thinking about a surfing theme for when the UK Championships are on. Most customers know who Keaton is and they know he's got through to the championships, so we should have a beach theme or something like that."

"Ooh, we could have sand, surfboards, and inflatables hanging from the ceiling. I can picture it now!" Scarlett says, getting excited.

"Are you going to stream the championships? They start early and last all day," I say.

"Yeah, of course we will. We need to get cover for the

bar. Eddie will take over as management and then we can get another couple of people in to help us out," Hunter says.

"Are you all coming to watch?" I ask. I assumed some of them would, but not all of them. I don't think we've all been away from the bar at one time before.

"Of course we are," Zac says. It's like he's angry that I thought they wouldn't come. "It's not every day your brother makes it through to the finals of the UK Championships. We're proud of you."

Wow. I don't think I've ever heard him say something as nice. "Thanks, man."

"Dinner's ready. You can carry on at the dining table," Dad says, carrying some bowls through. We all go into the kitchen and carry something over to the dining table and then we take our seats.

While we're eating, Dad asks, "So, Keaton, how is the surfing going? Are you getting ready for the championships?"

"Yeah, it's going. I'm at the beach nearly every day and I'm practicing and practicing. I'm in the gym every day for about two hours, then working at Mixology. I'm going to give Mixology a break if I get through the next phase because I need to clear my head and not have anything else to think about."

"Like Dakota Ryan," Zac says.

"I don't think about her. She's just in my way all the time. She's on the same beaches and turns up at the same time as me. I swear she's stalking me."

Everyone laughs.

"Are there other surfers there that are in the competition?" Skylar asks.

"Yeah. Why?"

Skylar laughs. "No reason. It's just you only ever talk

about Dakota, like you don't even notice anyone else there."

"Shut the fuck up!" I eat my Yorkshire pudding.

Everyone around the table laughs and starts tucking into their dinner.

DINNER with the family is always fun. It's light-hearted. We talk a bit about business and then we talk about ourselves and what we've been up to. I love those few hours that we all take time to make sure we have free. I love my family; they mean everything to me.

I finish getting ready and then jump in my car and drive to Mixology for my night shift. I know I get up early for surfing, but I love working at night. It's always busy, and before we know it, the night is over.

It's a busy night tonight and we don't stop. People want shots, cocktails, and lots of pitchers of beer. Must be a party night or something.

It's about ten-thirty and I swear to God I see someone who looks like Dakota Ryan in the queue for the bar. When I look again, she's gone. I bet she *is* stalking me, the bitch.

I serve another couple of girls who give me the eye and I bear them in mind for when it's time to go home. Then, when I turn to serve the next person, I'm faced with Dakota fucking Ryan. Except she's Dakota fuckable Ryan. She is smoking hot. I know I see her in a bikini more than anything and there isn't really much else that's smaller than that. But holy fucking smoke, she is gorgeous.

She has brunette hair which falls half way down her back in curls. She is slender as well as muscly and her make-up is perfect. The only fault is that she's swaying. She's as pissed as a fart. Shit. How am I going to handle this now?

"Heeey, Keeeeetoooon," she slurs. "Can I have a… a… Screaming Orgasm please?" She tries to keep a straight face.

I turn to make her the drink and I can feel my cock stirring in my pants. Now he wants to make an appearance? I don't need to be hard where she's concerned. She is staring at my arse when I turn around, and because now she can see my groin, she blushes when she sees the outline of my hard cock. "See something you like, Dakota?" I ask as I hand her drink to her.

"No. Just a horny man."

I lean over the bar. "I *could* give you a screaming orgasm." She gulps. "But I'm not going to. You can get your kicks somewhere else. Now, fuck off. I'm working and don't need you annoying me."

"This is a public bar and I am alllllllowwed to drink in here." She's a funny drunk. She stands with her hands on her hips, squaring up to me, but swaying at the same time. She shouldn't be drinking, she should be in training for the championship. Something must have happened for her to be drinking like this.

"You are allowed to drink in here. Stop annoying me." I don't want to tell her that she's making me laugh. She looks so cute.

She takes her drink, turns, and waltzes away, shaking her arse from side to side. The little bitch knows what she's doing.

I keep an eye on her all night and see she's attracting a lot of attention. A couple of times I go over to make sure she and her friend are okay and check if they need anything. At one stage, she grabs my leg and starts rubbing her hand up and down my thigh. My cock stirs and I try my hardest to think of the accounts or something that will help to bring him back down again. I don't want her to see what she does to me.

Towards the end of the night, she stumbles over to the bar. I try to ignore her and get Hunter or Eddie to serve her but, of course, they think it's funny to make me serve her.

"What do you want, Dakota? Don't you think you've had enough to drink already?"

"You're not my dad. Don't tell me what to do!" she spits. Guess I touched a raw nerve.

"Sorry. How can I possibly help you?" I ask, so very sweetly.

"I want more drink, please. I need it." She blinks away some tears. It does something to my stomach and I decide to back off a bit.

I make a couple of drinks for her and her friend and offer to carry them to her table for her. When I put the drinks on the table, she looks at me with her beautiful eyes and says, "Thank you, Keaton. I really mean it."

I smile, touch her on the shoulder, and walk back to the bar.

We start closing and Zac makes his way through the room, asking customers to drink up. He comes over as we're wiping down the bar and stacking the dishwasher. He leans over the bar.

"Hey, Keaton. Your girlfriend is falling asleep over there and her friends have left her."

"She's not my girlfriend." I stare at him.

"Well, she keeps saying your name." He laughs as he walks away.

I watch Zac clear the bar. He is so intimidating and I know if I was a customer I would leave when he told me to.

Dakota is in the corner and her head is bobbing. I walk

over and try to wake her up. She's not in a deep sleep, so I touch her on the shoulder and whisper in her ear. "Hey. Come on, sleepy head. Time to go home."

She stirs and opens her eyes. "Keeeaton. Take me home. Please."

"I don't know where you live. I know it's not close by. Where are your friends?"

"They left. I want you to take me to your house."

I shake my head. "No way. No one comes back to my house. Where were you supposed to stay?"

"Hotel. Seafront. Train station," she manages to get out.

"The Majestic? I'll take you back there."

"Will you take me to my room? I might get lost."

I laugh. Is she trying to get me alone in her room?

"Come on then. Let's go." I grab her hand and pull her out of the chair.

"See you later," Zac says with a smile on his face.

When we walk past Ainsley, she gives Dakota a hug and then looks up to me. "Look after her, Keaton. Don't take advantage of her."

"Do you really think so little of me that I would take advantage of a drunk woman?"

"No, but this is Dakota…" She holds her hands up in the air and does air quotes, "…'fucking' Ryan we're talking about."

"Fuck off, Ains." I start to walk Dakota out of Mixology and into the fresh air.

"Urgh. I don't feel well," she says.

I put my arm around her waist and pull her closer to me so I can take her weight. It's not a long walk, but I think it's going to take us a while.

"So, Dakota. Why did you come to Mixology tonight? It's way off your usual stomping ground."

"My dad's anniversary. I always get drunk. I wanted to see Scarlett."

"I'm sorry. When did you lose your dad?"

"It was five years ago. He had cancer. He was my hero. I miss him so much." She starts crying. I stop where we are and lift her onto the sea wall then step in between her legs. I pull her close and hug her while she sobs.

I know I'm a bastard, but I can feel my heart warm towards her a little. She's showing me her vulnerable side.

She sobs for a while then pulls back and wipes her eyes. "Thank you."

"What for? I haven't done anything."

"For helping me get back to the hotel."

"I'm a gentleman, regardless of what you think of me."

"I know you are." She tries to jump down from the wall. I help her and then we keep walking along the seafront.

The sea is rough and I can hear the waves crashing against the rocks and taste the salt in the air. It's a strange taste, but when you're in the sea as much as I am, you recognise it. I can feel the spray from the waves over us, and when the light mist lands on our arms, I can feel the salt on my bare skin.

We arrive at The Majestic and she gives me her room key. "Room 224," she says, and guides me to the lift.

We take the lift to the second floor and look for her room. I open the door and hold it for her to go in, then I put the key into the slot inside the door so the lights come on.

Following her into the room, I feel a bit awkward. I usually know what comes next when I go back to someone's room. Tonight, I haven't a clue what to do. Looking around me, I spot the kettle. "I'll make you a coffee."

I pick the kettle up and head into the bathroom to fill it

with water. When I come out, Dakota is laid on the bed with her dress hitched up over her arse. She must have tried to get undressed and fallen asleep.

Looking at her, my cock stirs again. I can see her thong. Wow, she really is gorgeous. Putting the kettle back down, I stare at her and think about making my exit.

"Keaton," she slurs. "Stay with me tonight." She can't even keep her eyes open. "Please."

Shit. What do I do now? There's no way I'm staying with her overnight. No way.

Walking over to the bed, I whisper, "Come on. You need to get undressed and climb into bed. You'll be cold if you sleep on top of it like that."

Suddenly, she reaches up and wraps her arms around my neck and kisses me. What the fuck? I try to pull away, I really do, but her kisses are addictive. So I do what any red-blooded man would do under the circumstances. I kiss her back.

After a few minutes of kissing me, I feel her start to go limp. I pull her dress off her and grab her t-shirt which she had left on the bed earlier, and put it on her. Before I do though, I take a good look at her body. She is fucking gorgeous. I shake my head before I think about staying. Once I have her tucked in the bed, I turn to walk away.

As I get to the door, I hear a small voice. "Keaton, I like you. I want you."

I don't listen to anymore. I open the door and walk out, leaving her there so she doesn't say anything else she might regret in the morning.

I smile all the way home when I think of Dakota and how I can tease her the next time I see her. Tonight turned out well in the end.

Tidal Wave

1/2 oz Gin, 1/2 oz Light rum, 1/2 oz Vodka, 1/2 oz Peach schnapps, 2 oz Orange juice, 2 oz Pineapple juice, 1 dash Grenadine syrup

I wake up at the crack of dawn and smile to myself when I think of Dakota. I can't wait to tease her about last night.

I need to get organised if I'm going to get to Watergate Bay early. I know for a fact that Dakota won't be there this morning; she was far too pissed last night. I won't be surprised if she doesn't turn up for a few days.

At Watergate Bay, I'm the only one surfing there. It's an amazing feeling when you're alone on the beach I feel the power of the sea and I love it. Two hours later, I head back home, desperate to jump in the shower again.

I'M MEETING my brothers and sister at Sea View for some brunch, so I jump into my car and drive down to Mixology and then walk to the café. They are all there waiting for me, drinking their coffees.

"What took you so long? Did you have a late night last night?" Zac asks, winking at me.

I should have known I would be in for some ribbing because I took Dakota home.

"No, it wasn't late. I was up early this morning."

"Didn't you stay for breakfast?" Hunter asks, laughing.

I hang my head. This is going to be a long brunch.

"I took her back to her hotel, put her to bed, and left her there." I don't tell them that she kissed me and told me she wanted me; they would only take the piss out of me.

"Did you take advantage of her? Get her out of your system?" Ainsley asks.

"God, not you too, Ains. I have enough from the lads, let alone you starting on me too." They all laugh. "She wasn't surfing this morning, so I assume she had a hangover. Which she deserves, I might add."

They're all shaking their heads at me. "Please don't mention it again," I say, taking up the menu, even though I know what I want.

"We've already ordered for you," Skylar says. "You always have the same."

I roll my eyes and take a deep breath. If I'd know how much they were going to take the piss, I wouldn't have come to meet them.

When the food arrives, they leave off me for a while and we talk about Mixology.

"Any news on Finn?" Zac asks Hunter.

Hunter sighs. "They sent him down for six months. Then he will be free to do whatever he wants. It sickens me. I'm sure he will come after us when he's out, but the police will be on alert."

"That's ridiculous. He beat you and Scarlett up and then only gets six months."

"That's our lovely judicial system for you." Hunter takes another sip of his coffee.

WHEN WE FINISH BRUNCH, we head next door to Mixology to start the stock take and see if there's anything we need to get for tonight.

Zac walks in after a while. "Look who I found knocking on the door."

We all turn and I'm sure I hear Ainsley laugh. It's Dakota Ryan.

"Hey, everyone," she says looking at the ground. I can see a blush crawl up her cheeks. When she lifts her head, she looks at me through her lashes. God, she looks hot. I see the moment she decides to pretend to be strong and confident. "Keaton, can I have a word please?"

I'm intrigued, so I grab her arm and guide her to the table by the front window. We both sit down. "What do you want, Dakota?"

"I want to apologise for last night. I was emotional and drunk, maybe even paralytic. I don't remember much at all, but I was dressed in my t-shirt when I woke up so I guess you undressed me and put it on for me."

She's blushing. Fuck, she looks gorgeous when she's embarrassed.

"I'd do that for anyone," I say, not meaning a word of it.

"I hope I didn't say anything embarrassing. I don't remember everything."

"No, you didn't. You told me about your dad and then you cried for a while. It's nothing. You didn't need to come in and say sorry."

23

"I'm polite, Keaton. I have manners and I know I was drunk and you looked after me. Thank you."

"You're welcome. I have to go back to work, so unless there is something else, I have to go." I stand.

She stands up too. "You're a prick, do you know that? I'm apologising and you have to be a dick about it. Fuck you, Keaton." She storms out of Mixology and down the seafront towards her hotel.

I hear someone clapping. It's Zac. "Well done. You managed to make her feel small and pissed off in ten minutes. Prick!" He walks away to carry some of the bottles into the bar.

I don't know why I was so mean to her. I didn't mean it. But she looked so cute that she took my breath away and I'm confused by my shift in feelings for her. I'll fight it all the way. She is my arch enemy; I can't like her. She beats me in competitions. I can't like her. She hates me.

I can't like her.

Throwing myself into getting Mixology ready for the punters tonight. I know that I'm going to be a whore tonight. I need to fuck Dakota fucking Ryan out of my system. Smiling, I go home to get ready to grab as many women as I can. I'm going have lots of 'breaks' in the office.

EXCEPT IT DOESN'T TURN out that way. No. Because I can't get Dakota fucking Ryan out of my head. Not at all. The bitch has taken her place front and centre in my mind and I feel so terrible for what I said to her. I'm trying to flirt with all the women; I don't even care what they look like at this stage. I just want one, or two. I don't care.

"Hey, gorgeous," I hear someone say. Turning, I see this amazing-looking woman. She's brunette, like Dakota.

She has a banging figure, just like Dakota. She is gorgeous and she is smiling at me.

"Right back at ya, babe. What're you looking for?" I flash her a smile.

"Can I have a Sloe Comfortable Screw, please?" she asks, winking at me.

"You can have any type of screw you like, sweetheart." I lay it on thick and she giggles. What is it with giggling girls? Dakota giggled last night and the sound went straight to my cock. Guess what? It doesn't tonight.

I make her drink and she hands me her phone number. "Call me later when you want that screw." Could she be any more obvious? I love it!

"Definitely. Catch you later." I turn and serve the next gorgeous customer.

Two hours later, I still can't get Dakota out of my mind. When we leave, I don't ring that girl. I don't ring anyone. I don't fuck anyone and I don't even get a fucking blowjob. I'm going to kill Dakota the next time I see her.

Hurricane

1/2 oz Vodka, 1/2 oz Gin, 1/2 oz Light rum, 1/2 oz Gold rum
1/2 oz Almond liqueur, 1/2 oz Triple sec, 2 oz Orange juice, 2 oz
Pineapple juice
Splash Grenadine syrup

When I wake up today, I can hear the waves crashing against the cliffs. I love the sound; it reminds me how nice and cosy it is in my house and in my bed. Then I remember that I need to practice today and big waves are hard to find in this country, so when I hear them, I need to act on them. I jump out of bed and flick the coffee machine on. Getting dressed, I get excited when I look out at the sea. It's really rough. Hopefully, it won't be so bad at Watergate Bay; that's where I'm headed today.

I make my coffee and bring an extra flask with me just in case I want some after my surf. I grab my towel, wetsuit, board, and some dry clothes then walk out to the car. I put my board in the top box on the roof and set off. It's dark out and I can feel the wind as I'm driving. I think about kissing Dakota and smile. It's such a good feeling. I hope she's not down here today, but then again, if she wants to spoil my morning surf then I'm going to fucking annoy her.

It takes me almost two hours to get there this morning. After parking up, I grab my stuff and run down to the shore. I change into my wetsuit and turn as I feel someone watching me.

"Spying on me, are you?" Dakota shouts in the wind.

"More like you're spying on me. Come for some lessons, have you?"

"I only learn from the pros. Oops, sorry, you're not one of those yet!" She grabs her board and runs into the sea.

It looks a bit choppy out there so I watch her run into the waves and then she jumps on her board and paddles out past the break in the waves. She jumps on her board and rides back into the shore.

I can't help watching her. She is an amazing surfer; not that I would tell her that. She is so graceful and looks beautiful out there.

"See something you like?" she shouts, goading me.

"Not really." I run past her into the crashing waves.

It's my time to show her what I'm capable of and she watches me paddle out and then surf back in again.

It's like a competition between us; who can stay on the board the longest. I think this is the first time we've stayed in each other's company for more than an hour.

I don't know how long we've been here, but we're pushing each other every time we go out. We go out farther each time and pick the biggest waves.

We both make it back to shore and I share my flask of coffee with her. She doesn't say anything, and nor do I. As soon as we've warmed up, we run to the waves and start all over again. It's been a long time since I've spent this much time in the water apart from during a competition. I'm not going to lie, I'm having fun.

It's mid-afternoon and we're both getting tired, but neither of us wants to quit before the other. We paddle our boards out farther than we've paddled all day. Each time we've been getting farther and farther away from shore. The sea is getting rougher, but it's nothing we can't handle.

The clouds are getting darker by the minute and I can feel the dampness in the air; it's about to lash it down. We stop and look at the shore before we paddle into the waves and jump on our boards.

This is one of those moments that's perfect. The waves are huge and you can ride on them with no difficulty. I'm shouting into the sky with my head held upwards. I can hear Dakota shouting too. She's shouting my name. I love the way it sounds coming from her mouth. I shake my head and concentrate on getting back to shore.

When my board comes in close enough, I jump off it and punch my fist in the air. "YES!"

I can't see Dakota anymore. Where the fuck is she?

The waves are huge at this stage and I have to wait a moment to see if she's on one of the bigger waves. But she's not.

I start to panic and then I see her beautiful hair. The next minute, it's gone. Without any thought to my own safety, I run into the water and throw myself down on my board. I paddle like my life depends on it. Where the fuck is she?

I see her head above the water, but she's moved in a different direction. If she's doing this to piss me off then I will fucking kill her. I change direction and she's getting closer.

"Dakota!"

She's disappeared under the waves again.

I roll off the board and dive down to see if I can see her. Opening your eyes under water stings like a bitch. I'm used to it though so it doesn't hurt as much. At this moment though it's just something that I need to do. I can see something to my right. I change direction and swim over. It's Dakota and she is fully submersed. I don't hesitate. I grab her and start kicking with all the power I have and more.

When I get to the surface, I take a deep breath. She doesn't. Shit. Where's my fucking board when I need it?

I see it and lay her on her back and drag her with me. I can feel myself getting tired but I keep going. Dakota needs me to keep going. When we get to my board, I try to lift her onto it, but I don't have the strength, so I manage to get her to hang over the board and I stay behind her to make sure she doesn't fall off. I kick with all my might.

Looking around, I see it will be quicker and easier to get to the little island off the bay rather than back on the shore because we've drifted so far out. Without thinking, I kick and kick until we eventually land on a small cove on the island.

Dragging my board up onto the beach, I lay Dakota on her back and try to wake her up.

"Dakota. Wake up. Dakota." She doesn't flinch or move a muscle. My lifeguard training comes into my mind and I lay her head back so her airway isn't obstructed. I pinch her nose, lay my lips over hers, and blow. Her chest rises so I let go, put my hands together, and press down on her breast bone. One. Two. Three. Shit. How many do I have to count to? I can't remember. Ten. Eleven. Is it fifteen or thirty? I can't remember. Shit! Fifteen. Sixteen. Time seems to be going so slow. What am I going to do if she dies? I can't let her die.

Twenty-four. Twenty-five.

Twenty-nine. Thirty.

I move back to her head, pinch her nose, and breathe into her mouth. Still nothing. I breathe into her mouth again. Moving back down to her chest, I start compressions again. One. Two.

"Come on, Dakota. Come on. Who am I going to argue with if you don't make it? Come on."

Twenty. Twenty-one.

I know that she could be brain damaged if she stops breathing for ten minutes or more. I don't know how long I've been doing this.

Twenty-nine. Thirty.

Moving back up to her mouth, I tilt her head and hold her nose. I wrap my lips around hers and blow. I take my mouth off and then lean back down and blow again.

Nothing happens.

Absolutely fucking nothing.

Dark 'N' Stormy

2 oz dark rum, 4 oz ginger beer, ½ cup ice

I can't believe it, but I start fucking crying. She's limp in my arms and all I can do is cry. I pull her close to me and hold her tight. My tears splash down onto her face.

Suddenly, I feel her body convulse and warm water on my chest. I roll her out of my tight grip and she starts coughing and choking.

"Oh my god, Dakota. You're alive. I don't fucking believe it."

I reach down and touch her cheek, and when she stops choking and spitting up seawater, her eyes glaze over and she looks at me.

"Keaton. What happened?"

"Ah, baby. You scared the shit out of me. You disappeared and I thought you were messing with me. I couldn't see you and when I paddled out to you, you kept disappearing. When I found you, I had to drag you onto the board and then it was easier to pull you here than go back to shore."

She looks around, noticing for the first time where we are.

"I had to… erm… resuscitate you." I feel myself blushing.

"Really? Oh my God." She starts to cry.

I pull her in close to my chest and hold her while she sobs. I run my hand up and down her hair, caressing her. Just keeping her safe.

"Tha… Thank you," she manages through her sobs. Her arms wrap around my back and she squeezes me with all her might.

"You'd have done the same for me." I can't explain how relieved I am.

We're both quiet for a long time. Then she asks, "Keaton?"

"Yeah?"

"How are we going to get to shore? We've only got one board and it's really rough." She looks out at the sea.

I look around and see the waves are crashing on the rocks and the sky is getting darker. "I think we need to try and get some shelter. We might have to stay here for the night. Are you okay? I need to look around the island and see if there is anywhere we can sleep." I start to move her off me.

"No! Don't leave me." She starts crying. "Please, Keaton. Don't leave me yet."

"Okay. Don't worry." I pull her closer to me again and hold her tight.

After a few minutes, I say, "What about if you see if you can stand and then we can look together."

She nods her head. I move her out of my way and stand up, then I grab her hand and pull her up. She wobbles a little and falls into my side. I look down at her and she looks up and says, "Sorry." Then she looks back down to the ground. God, she's gorgeous.

I put my arm around her shoulder and pull her close. I tell myself it's to keep her steady, but I know really it's because I want to protect her and keep her safe.

"Come on. Let's see if there's anywhere to sleep tonight. Hopefully the storm will blow over during the night and then we can paddle back to shore."

We wander around the small island until we find a cave on the opposite shore. It's not big but it will be big enough for the two of us to huddle together and keep warm.

"I think this might work. We can get some of the leaves and make a makeshift blanket. Unfortunately, neither of us has a towel or enough clothes to take off."

"Trust you to think about getting naked." She huffs.

"I meant if we had jumpers on then we could dry them off and lay them over us to keep us warm. But now you mention getting naked …" I pull her closer to me.

Luckily, she laughs. That's what I wanted to do. Break the tension in the air.

"Right, we need to find some wood and leaves to start a fire and that will keep us warm. We can light it just outside the cave and that way it can be seen by any ships passing."

"Do you have a lighter? You know to light this fire?" she asks sarcastically. "Surely it would be wet."

I laugh. "You are so lucky you're stranded with the Torquay Scouts survivor badge champion. If you were to *ever* be stranded with someone, then it's me. It's your lucky day, Dakota."

She starts laughing. "You were in the Scouts?"

"Yeah, I was. What's so funny about that?"

"I just got a mental image of you in navy blue shorts

and a top with a tie and a woggle. You are going to have to pull off something amazing to make that image disappear."

"Challenge accepted." I let her go and she sits on a rock. "You just stay there for a few minutes and let me see what we're dealing with here."

"Please don't leave me, Keaton," she whispers. "I'm scared."

I kneel down in front of her and take her hands. "Dakota. I'm not going to leave you and I'm not going to let anything happen to you. I promise."

She nods so I get up and walk around to see what we can use for firewood.

I'm only gone for about fifteen minutes when I find some big branches, and some ferns that have large fronds we can use to cover us overnight. Going back to Dakota, I take a couple of minutes to watch her. She looks so vulnerable sitting there looking around, trying to find me. She's so beautiful and I realise I've been pushing her away all this time because my feelings for her scare me. When I thought she was dead, it was like my life stopped.

"Hey, do you think you're up to helping me with some ferns? I could do with the help bringing them back."

"Of course," she says, standing and walking over to me. "Lead the way, boy scout." She smiles at me and it takes all my willpower not to lean down and kiss her. I remember when my lips were over hers, trying to save her life. I remember how soft and plump they were. I remember what they felt like the other night when I took her home. I shake my head and take her hand to guide her back to where the ferns are.

We spend a while picking the ones to use for covers. They're denser and more like blankets. We carry them to the cave and then go back to look for firewood. The sky is dark and it's getting hard to see. I can feel the first drop of rain and know it's going to absolutely lash down again. We run back to the cave for cover.

We just make it before it starts raining and I get some of the rocks and make a sort of small pool. I put some ferns in the bottom and watch as it starts to fill up. We need to drink fresh water or we're going to dehydrate. It will have to do for now.

Dakota takes the ferns into the cave and uses one of them to brush the floor so it isn't so rocky and then she lays a good amount down to give us something soft to lie on. In the meantime, I try to remember how to make a fire. It was one of the things I was good at when I was twelve, but now I need all the luck I can get. Today has been shitty and I hope that someone is looking down on me as I start to rub the stick between my hands and roll it back and forth as it rubs against another stick. There are some dry leaves underneath and all I'm hoping for is one spark.

After ten minutes, I get frustrated. "Why isn't this working? For fuck's sake." I lean my head back and look up into the sky. I would love to be in my house, looking out at this. It would be epic. But being here is a ball ache I don't need.

"Please. Please just work!" I shout up to the heavens. The next minute, I see smoke coming from the small pile of leaves on the ground. I move slowly so I don't put it out and gently blow to put some oxygen into it. When I see a flame, I put some more dry leaves and some of the wood that we brought back on it.

"Oh my God, Keaton. You did it. You fucking did it," Dakota shouts from inside the cave. She comes out and wraps her arms around my neck from behind. "I think I love you," she says. "You've saved my life twice today."

I laugh. "I was saving mine this time."

She pushes me. "Take a fucking compliment when it's handed to you."

"Sorry. I'm just not used to you being nice to me, that's all. All we ever do is wind each other up."

She turns and walks back into the cave. I guess this is going to be a long night.

6

Lost Bikini

1 oz Rum, 3/4 oz Galliano liqueur, 3/4 oz Almond liqueur, 1/2 oz Lime juice, 2 oz Mandarin juice

After making sure the fire is big enough to keep us warm, I head into the cave to face the wrath of Dakota.

"Look, we need to get on while we're here. It's only one night. I'm sure we can manage to be nice to each other for just one night. I was joking when I said I was saving my life."

"I know. It's just I get nervous in your company."

"Nervous. You?" I laugh. "You and nervous should never be in the same sentence. You're so confident and good at what you do."

She laughs. "It's an act." She sits down on the 'mattress' and crosses her legs, so I sit down beside her. "You're amazing at surfing and I feel like I have to try and keep up with you all the time." She looks to the floor and starts twisting one of the fronds. "Sometimes it takes a lot of hard work to keep up with you."

"Are you messing with me? You are so much better than me at surfing. I'm the one who hangs on your coat-tails all the time. You're the one person I have to try and beat and I never know if that's going to happen."

She leans against me. "Can we call a truce for tonight?"

I laugh. "I thought we had. I saved your life and you made me a bed." I throw my arm around her and pull her close. I don't want to argue with her anymore. Life is more precious than that. I kiss the side of her head; it feels so natural. She moans and leans in.

My cock stirs. I can't help it. That noise coming from her mouth is just so amazing. I want to hear it again.

The rain is coming down hard. The wind is howling and I can hear the waves crashing against the rocks. I have no idea what time it is, but I'm wrecked.

"I think we should try and sleep, Dakota. It's getting late and we've both had an exhausting day. You really need to see a doctor when we get out of here tomorrow."

"Yeah, I'm tired. I think I might take some of that water and then lie down."

I let her go and stand up. "I'll get it for you. I am a barman, after all."

I go outside the cave and find the fresh water which has fallen. There are a couple of big leaves so I bend them to use as a scoop and bring it in to her. I kneel down in front of her and hold the leaves out. She leans forward and gently sips the water out. She looks up at me and I can't take it anymore. I need to have her lips against mine. When she takes her final sip, I throw the leaves to one side to use later and then tip her chin up to look at me and lean closer. "Dakota," I say, and then I kiss her.

She doesn't even hesitate. She kisses me right back. Her

arms wrap around my neck and she pulls me down next to her.

This is the most amazing kiss ever. I don't think in all my life I have kissed anyone this perfect. Her tongue thrusts inside my mouth and meets my tongue beat for beat. I groan and pull her closer to me. She wraps her legs around my waist. God, I want her so bad. But I'm not an arsehole. I know our emotions are all over the place. We have to survive the night.

I pull away first. She smiles at me and blushes. I smile back and pull her into a hug. "God, that was good," I say. "Who'd have known it would be that good? We should have done that long ago instead of fighting all the time."

She giggles. She actually fucking giggles. "I've wanted to do that for ages, I just didn't want to admit it."

"You did admit it the other night when I took you to the hotel and put you to bed. I wanted to climb inside you and stay the night. But I thought I'd better be a gentleman and not take advantage of you in your drunken state."

"I wish you had," she whispers.

"You wish I had what?" I ask, wanting to hear her say it.

"I wish you had crawled inside me. I want that so much, Keaton. I want you so much." She faces me, reaches out, and runs her hand gently down my side, outlining my muscles. She reaches the 'V' and I take a deep breath.

"Dakota," I whisper. I don't know what I want to say. I just know I don't want her to stop.

She traces down the 'V' and slips her hand inside my board shorts. I hold my breath. She looks up at me before she wraps her delicate hand around my hard, hot cock.

She licks her lips. Fuck, I need to taste them again. I bow my head and take her lips in mine. I nip at her bottom lip and the most beautiful sound comes from her mouth.

Her groan makes my cock jump in her hand. She tightens her grip and pulls her mouth away from mine.

"I want to taste you, Keaton." She pushes me onto my back and straddles me. Strangely, it's only at that time that I realise how slight she is. I'm going to break her into pieces when I fuck her the way I want to.

She makes her way down my body, licking and kissing, while I run my fingers through her hair. I can't wait to grab that while I fuck her from behind. In my head, I can see all the things I want to do to her.

She pulls my shorts down and my cock springs into life and positions himself right where her mouth is. He knows what he wants more than I do.

Dakota looks up at me one last time for approval before she wraps her hot mouth around my hard cock.

"Fuck, Dakota!" I shout. "Don't ever stop that. God, it feels so good."

Her head keeps bobbing up and down my cock and she gags a few times. Even though I don't want her to gag, it sounds fucking amazing. She's like a porn star. I don't want to shoot my load early, so I grab her head and pop my cock out. Then I drag her up to me, kiss her, and then flip her over so that I'm on top and in charge of what happens next.

"Fuck," she says, wincing.

"Shit, did I hurt you? I forgot this isn't a nice soft bed. Where does it hurt?" I ask, reaching out to touch her everywhere.

She giggles. "It hurts here." She grabs hold of her tits and squashes them together. They're not huge, but they look fantastic trussed up in that triangle bikini. "And here," she says, reaching her hand down to her pussy. "It really hurts here." She looks up at me innocently.

"Oh, really? Well, then I'm going to have to make sure

those areas have extra attention." I kiss her and then move down her body like she moved down mine. There are kisses, licks, and nips. Talking about nips, when I get to her tits, I reach around her neck, untie her bikini, and pull it down.

"Fuck, Dakota. I don't think you realise how beautiful you look right now. You're looking at me like someone in ecstasy."

I lean over, take one of her nipples in my mouth, and flick it with my tongue. All the time I'm watching her I can see the emotions running over her face.

"I am in ecstasy, Keaton. Your mouth is so talented."

I take her nipple and nip it.

"Fuck!" she shouts. "Do it again."

I chuckle. My little spitfire likes a bit of biting. I store that away for next time.

What the fuck? I'm already thinking of next time and this one hasn't even finished. I don't fuck women more than once because they assume we're in a relationship. Then again, I haven't even fucked her yet and I know I want a next time.

I've made my way down to her bikini bottoms and she leans up on her arms to watch me. I take the side and am about to yank them apart when she shouts, "Stop!"

Shit. Has she changed her mind? "What the fuck, Dakota? You scared me then. Everything okay?"

"Don't rip them. I don't have anything else to wear when we go back after the storm."

I chuckle. "I forgot about that. Lift your arse then, because I'm thirsty and want your pussy."

She giggles and lifts her arse obligingly. I drag her bottoms down and throw them to the side somewhere. I lay down between her legs. Yes, it's uncomfortable. No, I don't care.

I reach up and open her lips and then slide my tongue in between them. She tastes good.

"Oh my God." She throws her head back.

I continue licking her and then I slowly insert one finger. She's tight. She bucks her body. I flick my tongue over her clit and she moans. I take my finger out and then insert a second one.

She starts to pant and I know she's trying to keep an orgasm at bay. "Dakota, let go. I want to see you let go." I lean down and suck her clitoris at the same time as finger fucking her.

She starts to tighten her body and I know she's close. I flick her clit again and it sends her spiralling over the edge.

"Keaton. Fuck!" Her shouts echo around the cave. I don't care if everyone in Torquay can hear her; it's the nicest sound in the world.

I slow my pace, and when she's back to Earth, I make my way up her body, plunge my tongue in her mouth, and devour her. "Taste yourself. It's delicious." Then I kiss her like my life depends on it.

She pulls away. "Keaton. I want you inside me. Please."

"I don't have any condoms. I didn't expect this would happen."

"I don't care. I'm on the pill and I'm clean. I don't have sex without condoms."

"But you're willing to with me?" On one hand, it makes me feel special. On the other, I know it's a stupid thing to do. But then again, I'm not using my head to think, I'm using my cock.

"Oh God, yeah. I want you inside me so bad. Please?" she says, looking up at me with doe eyes. Fuck. I'd give her anything right at this moment. Then she reaches down and grabs my cock. That's me done. I can't deny him what he wants. I take my shorts off and throw them in the same direction as her bikini bottoms and then position myself above her.

"Are you sure? This is your last chance. Once I'm inside it will be hard to pull out and stop. Please don't do that to me. I don't know if I can handle it."

She smiles. "Keaton, stop talking and just fuck me already."

That's enough for me. I line my cock up with her pussy and push the tip inside. Then, in one thrust, I push him all the way in.

"God!"

"No. Just me, baby." I wait for her to stop clenching my cock so hard. "Baby, you need to relax a little here or I'm going to go off like a little virgin."

She loosens her muscles enough for me to start moving. I move slow at first so she can get used to my width and then I can't help myself, I take her legs, push them back, and start fucking her with abandon.

I know I'm not going to last long. She's hot and tight and has the best pussy I've ever been inside. "Keaton, I'm going to come again." She pants.

"Fucking come all over my cock, Dakota. I want to watch you when you do."

So she does and, by God, it's the best thing I've ever witnessed. So much so it sends me over the top. I can't help myself. I empty my load inside her. I forgot to pull out, but at this moment in time, I really don't care.

When we're finished, I lie on top of her and kiss her.

LYING beside each other a little while later, Dakota wraps herself around me to keep warm. "Keaton?"

"Yeah?"

"Can we do that again sometime?"

I chuckle. If that isn't the best question I've heard for a long time.

"Don't you worry your pretty little head about that, Dakota. This is not a one-time thing we've got going on here." I kiss her. I just want to be as close to her as I can get.

"Keep me warm, Keaton. You make me feel safe."

"You are safe. I'll always keep you safe. Come here." She rolls away from me and then backs up so my body is wrapped around her, keeping both of us warm. I pull a couple of the big ferns over us and we somehow fall asleep. I feel like I've been sailing around the world and have just come home.

Dakota feels like home.

7

The Shifting Sands

1 ½ oz Beefeater Gin, 2 tsp Maraschino Liquer, 1 ½ oz grapefruit juice, ¼ oz fresh lemon juice, club soda

I'm cold. My back is freezing, but my front is boiling hot. What the hell? My bed feels hard. I open my eyes and the first thing I see is Dakota looking up at me, smiling. I smile back at her and she leans forward tentatively and kisses me chastely on the lips.

"Morning," I say. "Did you sleep well in this five star resort I brought you to?"

She laughs. "Well, I think the bed could do with a bit more cushioning. Other than that, I slept really well. There was something hard poking me this morning. Could be a spring or something." She looks up at me through her lashes.

Smiling, I reach down and adjust my hard cock. What is this girl doing to me? It's like she's taken hold of me and cast a spell over me. "We need to think about trying to get back to shore," I say, not really wanting to think about reality right now.

She slowly lies back down and looks at the roof of the cave. "Do we have to go right now?"

"I don't hear the wind and rain so I'm guessing the weather is better. People will be worried about us Dakota."

"I know. It's just…"

I grab her and roll her towards me so I'm lying on my back and she's tucked into my side, her head resting on my chest.

"It's just what?"

"What happens when we go back to shore, Keaton? What happens to us? Is this just a fantasy because you thought I was going to die?" She can't look me in the eye.

"Dakota. I told you last night that this is not going to be a one-time only offer. You're worth more than one night. Do you think I'm going to ignore you when we get home?" She doesn't say anything. "Do you?"

"Yeah. I thought you'd fuck me and then desert me as soon as we touch the sand. That's the reputation you have and you know it." She's looking down at the ground. Her voice has gone timid like she's very unsure of herself. She's usually such a confident person that I realise that she's feeling vulnerable. I've made her feel like that. That sucks.

"I know I do. But you're different. You were already under my skin, but now I've been inside you, there's nowhere I'd rather be."

She smiles wickedly at me. "Good." She climbs on top of me and straddles me. "Because I want you to be inside me right now." Knowing I'm already hard, she positions herself above my cock, grabs it with her hand, and slides down it slowly until she's fully seated.

"Dakota. Oh, that feels so good."

"You think people can wait a while before we go back to land?" she asks as she moves up and down.

"I think they'll wait another day if this is what you're going to do to me." I let her lead the way for a while and then she starts getting tired so I grab her hips and start pumping inside her. Fuck, she feels good. Having sex with Dakota feels better than anything I've ever experienced before. She fits me like a glove and the emotions I feel are something else.

"Keaton! I'm going to come."

"Let it go, babe. Give in to it," I say as she throws her head back and starts screaming my name. Fuck, that turns me on even more. When she starts to come down from her orgasm, I lay her down on my chest. "Hold on tight. I'm going to fuck your pussy hard."

She smiles up at me and then kisses me gently on the lips. I raise my knees and then start fucking her.

"Oh my God, Keaton. Yes, just like that. Harder. Fuck me harder."

She doesn't need to tell me again. I slam my cock in and out of her pussy. I'm sure we will both have bruises later. Just as I'm about to start my orgasm, she squeezes her muscles around my cock and calls my name. I lose it there and then. "Dakota, fuck." I think I'll get dehydrated from the amount of cum I lose inside her.

She flops back down on my chest. "Keaton. I don't want to give that up. Please keep me." She sounds so vulnerable.

"Dakota, you're my little spitfire and I don't intend to give you up. No fucking way can I go one day without being inside you. When we get back to land, I'm taking you to have a check up to make sure you're okay and then I'm dragging you back to my place. I don't think I'll let you leave for a while." I reach down to her face and bring her up to kiss her.

After several minutes, we unravel ourselves and look for our clothes. When we're ready, I take her hand and we head over to where we abandoned my board last night. The rain has stopped. The wind has calmed down and we can see the shore in the distance.

"Come on, babe. We can make it. You're not scared to get in the water, are you?" I turn to her. I hadn't thought about that before.

She smiles. "Are you kidding me? I live for the sea."

"I know you do, as much as I do. I just wanted to make sure after yesterday."

"Come on, my hero. Take me home."

We get into the sea and she lies on my board and grabs it from behind and then we paddle. She uses her arms and I kick my feet, like the perfect partnership.

It feels like it takes us hours to get back to shore, but I'm sure it's a lot quicker than that. We're both exhausted by the time we land on the beach and just roll onto our backs to catch our breath.

"Oh my God. Keaton. Dakota. You're okay." I hear my mum shouting as she runs down the beach, closely followed by Dakota's mum."

We both stand up and hug our mothers, even though they'll get wet. It's so good to see them. Dakota starts crying and I want to grab her and hold her, but her mum doesn't let her go.

"What happened? Actually, let me ring Hunter first and tell him you're okay. He's gone with Zac and Ainsley to get Dad's boat to go looking for you."

Mum rings Hunter and Skylar. Apparently, he's trying to track us using satellite technology. What he doesn't know about technology is not worth knowing.

Our mums have towels and they wrap us up in them and my mum asks again what happened.

We tell them about the sea and how rough it was and how Dakota disappeared. I find myself getting emotional thinking about how close she was to dying. I can't help myself, I take her from her mum and hug her. I kiss her on the head. "I had to give her mouth to mouth to bring her back and I pumped on her chest until I thought she had died." A lone tear runs down my face. The thought of her dying kills me.

Dakota continues. "When I started breathing again, he held me and looked after me. He made a fire. He got ferns for a mattress and for cover. He found a cave for us to shelter in last night." She turns to my mum. "If it wasn't for your son, I'd be dead and at the bottom of the sea." She looks up at me, begging for a kiss. I can't help myself. I lean down and kiss her gently.

"Finally!" both mums shout.

I look at them. "What?"

"You two got together, finally," Dakota's mum says. "I'm sick of hearing how much she hates you." I look at Dakota and she blushes.

"Yeah, and I'm sick of hearing about Dakota fucking Ryan," Mum says, and Dakota looks at me.

I shrug and say, "Sorry." We both start laughing.

"I guess being faced with adversity makes your true feelings come out," I say, pulling her in close again.

"Yeah. We only have one life. No point being unhappy," Dakota says, and squeezes me.

"Anyway, what are you guys doing here?" I ask Mum.

"When you didn't turn up for work, Hunter rang me to see if you were with us. When we couldn't contact you, we got Skylar to track your phone. Then we came down here and when we saw both your cars, we were worried. We found the flask in the sand and your phone in the car, and your car was unlocked. It was dark and stormy so the coastguard couldn't go out to see if they could see you. We've been worried sick. We called Dakota's mum and she came down with us. We waited here all night and as soon as the storm went and the sun came up, Dad went over to get the boat and look for you guys himself," Mum says, wiping her eyes.

Dakota's mum carries on. "We thought you'd both died. The waves have been crashing against all the rocks and cliffs and we thought there was no chance that you would make it out alive. We were so scared." She wipes her eyes too. "Keaton, thank you for saving Dakota's life. I'll always be grateful." She comes over and hugs me. I get embarrassed and blush.

"She would have done the same for me." I look at Dakota. "I hope."

She smiles at me. "You know I would."

"Right, we need to get you to hospital for a check-up, Dakota. Keaton, do you need to be checked over too?" her mum asks.

"No, I'm fine. I didn't swallow water like she did."

"We'll be having dinner this evening and would love you both to come along." Mum says, surprising me. I know our relationship is new, but I'm delighted that Dakota is invited to dinner.

"We'd love to, but it should be us making dinner for Keaton."

"Don't worry. I think we'll be seeing each other often enough." Mum smiles at me.

They start to make their way back to the cars and I stand next to Dakota. "Let me know how you get on at the hospital. I want to come with you, but I think you need some time with your mum." I pull her in and kiss her hard. She wraps her arms around my neck and pulls me closer.

Her tongue plunges into my mouth and wraps around mine. This is heaven. This is where I belong.

We finally pull apart and say goodbye. It hurts to watch her walk away. But I know it won't be long until I see her at Mum's.

We get back home and I take a warm shower. The feeling of the hot water hitting my back and warming my bones is one of the best feelings in the world. Well, next to being inside Dakota. Just the thought of her makes my cock stand to attention and I stroke him and think about her some more. I lean with my hand up high on the shower wall and the other one is squeezing my cock and rubbing one off.

I feel so much better after showering and putting on some dry clothes. When I walk into the lounge, all my family is there and Ainsley runs over and hugs me. "We all thought you were dead." She sniffles.

"Are you crying, Ains?"

"Yeah, you bastard. I thought you weren't coming back and I was looking forward to moving into your place." She laughs, her tears drying up instantly.

"Bitch!" I say, and move away from her, laughing.

I tell them everything that happened. Well, almost everything. Of course, they all want to know about Dakota.

She texts me and tells me that she needs to stay in hospital overnight for observation. Her blood pressure is low and she is slightly dehydrated so they can't come over for dinner. I don't care about that; I'm worried about her now. I'm going to visit her after dinner with the family.

The family is delighted that we finally got together. Apparently, they have all seen what the two of us didn't. I take a lot of ribbing, especially from Hunter and Scarlett.

She was so worried about the two of us that she threw herself at me when she saw me. I know I haven't known her long, but we've really clicked.

I love my family and I'm glad we made it back in one piece.

8

The Champion

1 slice orange, 1 slice lemon, ½ tsp grated fresh ginger, 1tb honey, 2 parts Bulleit Bourbon, 1 part sweet vermouth, 1 part dry vermouth, 2 dashes orange bitters, candied ginger for garnish

After dinner, I say goodbye, and instead of going home, I drive over to the hospital to see Dakota. They won't let me in at first, but I tell them that I drove almost two hours to get there and I saved her life yesterday. They eventually let me in and I feel like I'm walking on air. She's in her own room and I knock on the door and walk in. When she sees me, her face lights up. "Keaton, how did you get in?"

"I might have told them that I saved your life and I drove here two hours to see how you are. They felt sorry for me." I sit on the bed and take her hand. I kiss it and keep hold of it as I rest it back down on the bed. "So, how are you feeling?"

"I'm okay. My head hurts, but they said that's from dehydration. I don't suppose we drank enough of that water when we were... you know."

I smile. "You know? You mean when we were fuck-ing?" She blushes. I love that about her. She's innocent, but she's naughty.

"I think we might have been too pre-occupied to drink more water. It was fun though."

"It certainly was. So, when are they letting you out of here?"

"Hopefully tomorrow. They're happy with everything. I just need to be rehydrated. Why?"

"I want to know when I'm going to have you to myself again. Plus, I want to show you my house. I just know you're going to love it." I smile thinking about her in my house, looking at the little cove.

"Where do you live?" she asks.

"I'm not telling you. It will be a surprise." We sit there for a little while, not really saying anything, when the nurse pops her head in.

"You're going to have to leave now. Visiting hours were over a couple of hours ago and Dakota needs some sleep. She should be okay to go home after the doctor has been around in the morning." She leaves the room and closes the door.

"Do you want me to come and collect you?"

"I think Mum is coming. She's finding it hard to get over the fact that I nearly died. But if you want to come see me at home, you can."

I stand and move closer to her. Leaning down, I kiss her gently on the lips, but she pushes her way in and starts to kiss me like it's the last time. When she pulls away, she says, "I can't get enough of you, Keaton James. Why did we wait so long?"

"I think if we had hooked up before it would have been a one night hook up. At least we know how we feel isn't just a..."

"One time deal," she finishes for me, laughing.

"Yeah. I guess I said that quite a lot, didn't I?"

"You did, but it was nice to hear. I'll let you know when I'm home and then we can arrange something."

I kiss her one more time and then wave as I leave the room. Driving home, she is all I can think of.

A WEEK LATER, I wake up with Dakota wrapped around me and the sun blaring. She has stayed over most nights since that day, and we've surfed and trained together. Today is our first competition as a couple, which should be awkward, but it won't be. We're very evenly matched so will be happy as long as we both place in the top four because it means we can go to Byron Bay in Australia for the World Surfing Championships. This is what we have both been working up to all these years.

"Hey, babe. Wakey, wakey, rise and shine." I turn and kiss her cute nose.

She smiles at me. "Let me sleep."

Laughing, I climb out of bed and pull the duvet off her. It seemed like a great idea, but when I see her gorgeous naked body, I realise maybe it wasn't. Nope. I don't have time to take her now. It can wait until we know for sure we're both through to the World Championships.

"Keaton James, I am going to kill you for that." She jumps out of bed and tries to chase me around the house. I can't stop laughing at her trying to catch me. I slow down so that she does. I know what will happen.

She bangs into me and wraps her arms around my neck. "Come down here and give me a kiss."

So I do. Who am I to refuse a beautiful woman a kiss?

After we break away from each other, I pop the coffee machine on. Old habits die hard. We get dressed and stand at the glass doors, looking out at the sea like we do every morning, trying to assess the weather and the waves.

"It looks good out there, Keaton," she says. "I think I am definitely going to whoop your arse today." She laughs.

"Really? You think you're going to whoop my arse? Is that a challenge?"

"Maybe it is. Maybe we should put a bet on who is going to win." She looks defiant.

"Let's do it."

"Okay, when I win," she says, "I'm going to boss you around the bedroom for one night. You have to give up control to me."

"Oh, really? Well, when I win, I get to keep you forever," I say, shocking myself.

She blushes and mumbles something under breath and turns to walk away.

"What's wrong with that?" I ask.

"You don't mean that. You mean you get to keep me until you're fed up of me. I don't want to get into it now. We have to get ready for the competition." She turns to walk into the bedroom.

"Dakota, come back here." I reach out and take her arm. She turns slowly to face me. "What is going on in your pretty little head?" I ask as I pull her closer to my body. I wrap my arms around her and keep her from moving.

"I don't know. I just feel like this is all a dream and you're going to wake up and not want me anymore. I don't know if I could handle that." She won't look at me.

Putting my finger under her chin, I lift it up so that she has to look at me. "Babe, I worry that you're going to do that to me every day. I just try to make you see that life wouldn't be the same if we weren't together. I don't believe in all that romance nonsense, but since the other week, I want to do all of that stuff with you. I want you to move in. I want us to have kids. I want all of that. Remember, this is not a one-time deal. It's more than that."

She smiles and I lean down and kiss her. It's a kiss full of emotion and I don't want to stop, but know that we have to get ready to go.

She pulls away. "Come on, Romeo. Let's get ready and win this competition."

THREE HOURS LATER, the beach is packed with people in Watergate Bay, and the area for surfing has been cordoned off. Mum, Dad, and the family are seated in the VIP area with Dakota's mum. The VIP area is saved for the families of the competitors.

"Are you ready for this?" I ask Dakota. She is up before me and I can see she's getting nervous. It's funny; I never noticed that before. I always thought she was cocky and arrogant when it came to her surfing because she's so good.

"I'm always ready for surfing and a bit of friendly competition."

"You look nervous. I don't normally see you nervous."

"I never showed it around you because I thought you would laugh at me, so I was always pretending to be cocky." She smiles. "Everything feels different this time though. I love it."

"You hid it well." I kiss her on the cheek. "Now get over to the start and get yourself ready. Just remember, I'm going to kick your arse."

She laughs and walks away, shaking her arse from side to side as she goes. I'm nervous for her and excited at the same time.

She gets to the starting line and then gets into the water. She has to do five different moves and she is judged on how she does each of them. It's not easy and you have to judge the waves in a split second and decide which move you're going to make.

When she jumps on her board for the first time, we all shout her name and cheer her on. We clap when she lands back on the beach and I wolf whistle at her. She turns to look at me, smiles, and then jumps back in the sea to do the next one.

When she finishes, everyone goes mad. She has to have got perfect scores for each of those moves. But unfortunately, the judges didn't agree. They gave her lower marks for two of the moves. I never noticed anything wrong, but then in my eyes, she never does anything wrong. It's still the highest score of the day. We clap when she comes over. I wrap her in a towel and hold her tight.

"Well done. You did fantastic. You're top of the leader board, babe." I kiss her and hold her to warm her up.

"I dropped a couple of points though." She's clearly disappointed.

"Listen, someone has to get at least one point off full scores to beat you, and let's be honest, the rest of the surfers aren't a patch on you."

"Except you." She grins.

"Well, of course me. I think it's your turn to beat me this time. We seem to take it in turns."

"Well you saved my life, so I think it might be your turn." She's quiet for a moment. "As long as we both place in the top four, Keaton, then we can both go to Australia for the World Championships. It would be a dream come true, and to share it with you would be amazing."

"Even if only one of us places, we will still both be going to Australia. Do you think I'm letting you go over there without me? I've spent too long without you to let you disappear for a couple of months." I kiss her again and then I hear my name being called.

"It's your turn, Keaton. Maybe you should lose. I know you want to give me control in the bedroom for one night."

"Are you fucking kidding me? My part of the bargain is much better. I'd rather have you for life and then I can give up control anytime you want."

I make my way over to the starting line and give my name to the guy and then, when I'm told, I run into the sea. I hear my name being called and it spurs me on. Once I'm deep enough, I lie down on my board and paddle out past the really big waves. While I wait for the wave to come along and take me on my journey, I think about Dakota and how close I was to losing her. I miss the next wave that comes and realise I need to concentrate or she will be going to Australia without me.

The next wave comes along and as soon as I'm on it, it feels like I'm riding on top of the world. I can feel the power of the wave pushing my board. I feel like I'm gaining speed and the thrill is coursing through my body. Just as I crown on the crest of the wave, I feel the air whooshing past me, I hear the waves starting to break and the spray washes over me. I can't hear the crowds; they don't exist in this moment in time. All that exists is me and this wave.

As I land on the sand, I turn around with the biggest smile on my face and run straight back out to sea for the next one.

The feeling is almost spiritual and I'm at one with the sea. I can hear the sound of the seagulls as they circle above, watching to see if we stir up any fish.

When I land on the sand for the last time, there's a big cheer and I almost collapse. I put so much effort into it that I'm wrecked. It takes a minute for my scores to come up and I'm astonished that I get full marks across the board from all the judges. I turn to face Dakota and she's crying. I run over to her and she wraps me in a towel and dries me like I dried her.

"Oh my God, Keaton. I've never seen you surf as well as you did today. You were fantastic. I'm so proud of you." I hug her with all my might. How different today could have been if we were fighting as always.

"That was so much fun." I kiss her.

"Keaton." I hear my mum shouting. The two of us make our way into the crowds to where our families are sitting and we get lots of hugs and congratulations. The competition isn't over and we know the leader board could change at any minute, but we're enjoying these few minutes with those who love us.

"You were both amazing. I'm so proud of you both," Mum says, kissing us on the cheek.

We wait another hour for the last surfer to come home and then the leader board changes for the last time today.

First Place: Keaton James - Devon

Second Place: Dakota Ryan - Cornwall

Third Place: Paul Evans - Yorkshire

Fourth Place: Justin Hall – South East

Dakota jumps up and down. I think she's crying too. My family hugs both of us. Dakota's mum is crying and so is mine.

I hug Dakota and whisper in her ear, "I love you. I know we've only been dating for a short time, but we've been through so much together. I don't want you to not know how much I love you."

She turns to face me with tears in her eyes. "Really? I love you so much too."

I pull her close and hold her tight. "Remember my prize? Forever. Just hold that thought and don't forget it."

9

Epilogue

DAKOTA
Waking up in Keaton's arms is the best feeling in the world. He is so strong and such an amazing person. I'm almost embarrassed we waited so long to be nice to each other. I think we were so horrible to each other because, deep down, we liked each other. I will never forget what he did for me. He saved my life. How many people can say that the person they love the most in the world saved their life? I can and I do, regularly.

Today we're going to his parents' for Sunday dinner. They invited me after the accident, but I couldn't go, and I'm nervous. They've been in Keaton's house and I've seen them at the competition and such like, but I've never been in their house for dinner. At least Scarlett will be there.

Keaton and I grab our boards and run down to the little cove. I can't believe he lives in a house with its own cove. This is like a small slice of heaven and I'm so lucky to be living here with him. I haven't really gone home much since we met. It doesn't feel right not staying with him every night. We've been in serious training for the world championships in two months and haven't had time for much else.

After catching a few waves and messing around for a bit, we go back up to the house. I turn the coffee machine on and then go hit the shower. Keaton joins me and it delays us so we have to put the coffee machine on again. We take our coffees and sit out on the balcony, staring at the sea. This is our dream come true. Sitting here together, close to the sea.

After we've finished everything, we take the car and drive to his parents'.

Hunter and Scarlett are already there when we arrive. Thank God. Keaton takes my hand and squeezes it.

"You'll be fine. Don't look so worried." He kisses me on the cheek. He's so sweet. We go by the kitchen first to say hello to his parents.

"Hey, guys. Go sit down. Keaton, get Dakota a drink," his mum says.

He laughs. "Obviously." He takes me into the lounge and I sit on the couch next to Scarlett.

"Hey," she says. "How's the training going?"

"It's hard work. We're in the gym for a couple of hours a day and then out at sea every morning. Keaton is at Mixology at night. I think he's going to be taking some time off soon because it's wearing him out."

"Yeah, he looks tired," she says, nodding her head over to him. He's deep in conversation with Hunter and the two of them are laughing.

"Believe me, he is worn out."

"Yeah, but that's probably not from the gym," she says, smiling at me.

"So true."

Zac walks into the room. I'm not sure how I feel about him yet. He's very quiet, and not as friendly as the other

James siblings. He smiles at me and then joins the lads, but he just listens and doesn't talk.

Ainsley comes in, runs straight over to us, and sits next to me. "I'm so glad there are girls here now. I was getting lonely with just the boys."

We have spent some time together and the three of us get on really well. If I had a sister, I would love to have Ainsley. She is extremely passionate about Mixology and loves her brothers more than anything.

Keaton brings drinks for Ainsley, Scarlett, and me. "Got to keep the women lubricated," he says with a wink before walking away.

"I'm so glad you two got together," Ainsley says. "He's a different guy altogether. Whenever he gave out about you being the one to beat, we were all laughing at him. We knew he liked you before he did. It was hilarious."

"I was the same though. I knew he was a prick with the women so I didn't want to be one of his 'surf bunnies'. That's not what I'm about."

"Surf bunnies. Oh my God, that's hilarious," Ainsley says, laughing. "You are certainly not one of those. You're well matched and I know how competitive you both are. I can't wait to see how you do in Australia."

We sip our drinks. Then I ask a question that has been playing on my mind. "What's Zac's story? He's always so quiet unless he's throwing someone out of Mixology."

Ainsley looks over at Zac and then back to me. "Zac's story is sad, but it's his story, and when he knows you better, he'll share it with you. Sorry."

"It's okay. I just wanted to try and get to know him a bit better."

"He's a very loyal man. I get on with him best because the two of us work together at the front door most nights.

He shuts himself off from people though, so you should never take offence to him."

"Dinner's ready," their mum shouts from the kitchen. Everyone stands up and walks to the kitchen. That's strange; I thought we were going to eat at the dining table. It's all laid ready. I follow everyone and then see Hunter and Keaton coming out with dishes. I smile at Keaton as he passes. He winks back at me.

We all take one dish each and lay it on the table. This small move means so much. Every one of the James family has so much respect for their parents and they just proved it tenfold.

EVERYONE TALKS around the table about what has been happening since the last dinner. His mum even asked me what was going on in my life.

"Well, we've been training hard and getting ready for going to Australia."

"When are you thinking of going out there?" his dad asks.

I look at Keaton. "We're not sure yet. Keaton needs to decide when he can leave Mixology and then we need to look at flights and where we're going to stay. It would be expensive to go over too early and stay in hotels all the time. We've got about two months before the competition so maybe we will go out in a month's time." I smile at them and take a sip of my drink.

"Hunter, when are you looking at letting Keaton go?" their mum asks.

"It's not about me letting him go. He can leave anytime, he knows that. I know you don't want to let us down, buddy, but this is important for both of you."

"It's hard though. We're a family unit and I don't want to let you all down by leaving too early," Keaton says.

"Fuck off, Keaton. We are so proud of you, but you need to acclimatise and prepare," Zac says. I think that's the most I've heard him say.

"The reason I was asking is because I've been talking to a friend of mine who lives in Australia and she's going to rent us her summer house for the next three months. They live in Armidale which is a four-hour drive to Byron Bay and they're happy to let you move in there for three months." Keaton starts to say something. His mum puts her hand up. "I know you might not want to stay for three months. You might want to come back straight after the competition, but the choice is there if you want to stay. We might be able to come out and then we can all stay there. What do you think?"

She looks at the two of us.

"Mum, we can't afford to be off work for three months and pay rent. Thank you so much for thinking of us though." He smiles at her, takes my hand, and squeezes it.

"We're going to pay for it ..."

"No, we can't ask you to do that," Keaton interrupts.

"I know you would never ask. I don't think you realise how proud we are of you both. Not only is our son representing the UK in the World Surfing Championship, but so is his girlfriend," his dad says. "Of course we want to do whatever we can to help."

I feel tears in my eyes. This family is so thoughtful and amazing.

"Thank you so much," Keaton says. "That means it'll be easier for us to go earlier." He looks at me.

"I don't know what to say. Thank you. You're amazing," I say, meaning every word.

"Go home and start planning and then let us know and we'll arrange it with our friends," his mum says.

The conversation moves on and Hunter says to Zac, "So, Zac, if there's a pattern here then you're next to find a good woman."

"Stop it, Hunter. You should see how many times he gets hit on every night." Ainsley laughs. "He won't be settling down soon."

"I think you all forget I settled down before and it didn't work out well for me," Zac says, sounding pissed off.

"We know but, Zac, you're young. You can still have love in your life," Keaton says. "Look at me."

"No way. Not happening. I never want to give my heart away again. Why would I when I can have any woman every night of the week?" He smiles, and for the first time, I see how good-looking he is. When he's all gruff and moody, he looks sinister, but when he's laughing and joking, he is really gorgeous. Not my type, but gorgeous nonetheless.

"Yeah, but you don't. You just watch them come and go," Ainsley says, nudging him on the shoulder.

"Ah, but you don't know what goes on in my life when I leave Mixology." He looks at Ainsley. "Do you?" Then he smiles again.

Everyone starts laughing and Keaton leans over and whispers in my ear, "Ainsley thinks she knows everything about us, but she doesn't. Zac like to remind her every now and again."

The fun and laughter around the table at dinner is amazing and they make me feel so welcome, particularly as Keaton was always calling me names before we hooked up. I feel like a bona fide member of their family and I'm in shock at his parents' offer.

We make it back to Keaton's house in the early afternoon and he has a couple of hours before he has to go to work. I've been helping out behind the bar, just to get some extra money for Australia and to spend time with Keaton, of course.

"Come and sit outside," he says, and he grabs us both some coffee.

I follow him out and sit at the table, which is perfectly situated so we can see the cove below us. "How do you think dinner went?" he asks.

"I felt so welcome and I just love your family. They're so nice. I can't believe what your mum and dad are doing for us."

"It's good of them and I guess they want to come and watch the championship, which is awesome. Maybe we can get your mum to go over with them and she can see us in action too."

"Oh my God, that would be so good. She wouldn't travel all that way on her own so it might be the only way to get her out there."

I take a sip of my coffee. Keaton looks at me seriously.

"I know we've only been together a short while, but you know you're my forever, right?"

I blush. It embarrasses me when he says that because he doesn't do relationships and I know that. I know that there is a short expiry on our relationship, but I will take his love for as long as I can have it.

"I was thinking after the competition maybe we can stay an extra month and have a holiday. We'll need it after all the training we'll be doing over there."

"That sounds like a great idea. I love it."

"Seeing as you're my forever and we will have the opportunity of being in Australia together, alone for a period of time, I wanted to know what you think about us getting married on a beach out there."

I almost drop my cup. Married? He wants us to get married? "Keaton... I, erm... I don't know what to say. This is a bit quick, isn't it? Did you fall and bang your head or something?"

He laughs and gets down onto his knees. "Dakota. I've never felt this way before. I know what I want. If you need time, that's fine. Let's see how we get on in Australia and then we can have this conversation again." He reaches out, puts his two hands on my face, and brings me in close so he can kiss me. There is so much emotion in his kiss that it brings me to tears.

"I love you," he says when he breaks away from the kiss. "Hey. What are the tears for?"

"I love you too, Keaton. I'm crying because I'm so happy to have you in my life. I want you to be my forever too."

THANK you for reading KEATON as part of the Mixology Series. I really hope you enjoyed it and that you'll consider leaving a review on Amazon. It's a great way to help other readers discover new books.

Continue reading for a sneak peak of ZAC, the next book in the Mixology Series.

PROLOGUE

Where the fuck is she?

Erika is a designer, sometimes she gets carried away with a project and doesn't realise what time it is. She's always late for our dates. It makes me really mad. But I just can't stay mad at her for long. I love Erika. She is my soul mate and I would do anything for her.

I work in London at one of the large banks. My job is really stressful, so I always liked to play hard. However, since I met Erika and she moved in with me, the only playing I like to do is with her. It's our anniversary today and we've been together for three happy years.

I'm particularly eager for her to finish work tonight because I'm going to ask her to marry me. My beautiful, elegant, Erika, the love of my life and I can't wait to show her the ring that I have to seal the deal. You should see it. It's a huge, square diamond with smaller diamonds running down the neck of the platinum ring. Taking it out of my pocket, I look at it one more time, just to make sure I haven't dropped it on the way here. Yep, it's still there. I put it back in my pocket knowing the next time I take it out will be when I put it on her finger.

Having been a bit wild since I moved to London, I never thought I would settle down. Listen, I've been earning a lot of money working in the banking industry. It's pressurised so we let off a lot of steam after work. That means drinks, drugs and women. Lots of women.

I met Erika on one of those many nights out and she changed my perspective on relationships. She showed me how good it can be with someone you love.

Checking my phone one more time I get annoyed. She had better not have totally forgotten about tonight. I'm nervous and annoyed at the same time.

Dialling her number for the fourth time, I put the

phone to my ear ready to hear her excuses. It rings and rings and rings. No answer.

"Excuse me sir, do you want a drink while you're waiting." Someone says, breaking through my thoughts.

"Please, I think I'm going to need one. Can I have a bottle of sauvignon blanc, the most expensive you have please and a Courvoisier." He nods his head and moves away from the table.

Picking up the phone again I ring her number. She better answer this time.

"Hello ... Zac I'm sorry." She sounds out of breath. "I was just handing some work over. I know I'm running late, but I'm on my way. I'm just locking up now." She's panting so I know she is moving fast.

"Erika, just hurry up will you. I'm sitting her like a tit waiting for you. Everyone is looking at me like I've been stood up and you know how much that pisses me off. I wanted tonight to be special."

"I know Zac and I'm sorry. I'll make it up to you later on, I promise." She says seductively.

The smile spreads across my face. "How are you going to make it up to me baby?" We love playing this game. Because we both work long hours sometimes we sext each other. It keeps our relationship alive and it's great fun.

I can picture her smiling as she says, "Well the first thing I am going to do is reach under the table and feel your cock, give it a squeeze and then I'm going to take my knickers off and put them in my pocket. You're going to have to sit there while we have dinner and know that I am wet and ready for you."

"Erika, you're killing me."

"I'm going to do a lot more than that."

"I want you to tell me when you're in the back of the taxi."

"But he'll hear me." She says, expecting me to back down.

"Yeah I know, and that will turn me on even more. You owe me. I'm sitting here in this posh restaurant, on my own, waiting for the love of my life with a massive hard cock."

She laughs. I love that laugh. It makes me so happy when she laughs. "Okay, I'm all locked up lover boy. I'm coming to get you. Hang on, there's a taxi, I'm just going to put my hand up and grab it."

"That sounds like you're talking about my cock." I laugh.

"Wait a few more minutes, big boy."

I hear her shout "Taxi!" then I hear her running in her high heels.

All of a sudden I hear horns beeping, a scream and people shouting all at once.

"Fuck Erika, what's going on?" Nothing. Erika is the type of person who would stop and help someone if they fell over or needed some help.

"Erika." I shout again. I stand up and walk outside the restaurant, I don't want to be shouting for her attention in the middle of the place.

"Erika, tell me what's going on. Erika!"

I hear a commotion on the other end of the phone. Someone saying, "Ring an ambulance. She's in a bad way."

My heart starts racing and I start screaming down the phone. "For fucks sake Erika, answer the phone!" I need to know that my forever girl is okay and she is just helping someone else out.

There's some more shuffling and I keep calling her name. Next thing I hear her shuffling as she picks up her phone.

"Erika," I say relieved to hear her moving. "What's going on? Are you okay?"

"Excuse me, who is this?" I hear a gruff voice say. My heart drops.

"Where's Erika? Put her on the phone. Tell her I'm losing my life here. She's about five foot nine, she has brunette hair and she's …"

"I'm sorry, there was an accident. She's not able to come to the phone. Who are you?" The voice says.

"I'm her partner. What the fuck is going on?" I'm screaming down the phone now.

"She's been knocked over." The voice says with no empathy whatsoever.

"What? Oh my god, put her on the phone so I can talk to her. I can calm her down. I bet she's panicking."

"I'm sorry sir …." I hear some voices in the background and the sirens have stopped. It takes another couple of minutes before someone takes the phone and says, "Are you her boyfriend?"

"Yes I am. Can you tell me what the fuck is going on?" I'm getting to the point where I'm going to explode if they don't put Erika on the phone.

"Sir. Calm down. She's been involved in an accident and the ambulance is here. They are going to take her to St George's Hospital."

"I'm on my way."

"Sir, it's not looking good."

"What the fuck does that mean? I don't care if she has broken a leg or something."

"No sir, prepare yourself for the worst. We are prepping her ready to leave. Hurry and meet us there." He hangs up.

What the fuck does he mean, 'prepare for the worst'?

She was crossing a road for fucks sake. The cars don't move fast at this time of night.

I jump into a cab and ask him to get to the hospital really quickly.

I feel sick. My heart is pounding. I feel clammy. I'm confused, I just don't know what is going on. The traffic is quite heavy, so I get out of the taxi and run the rest of the way. When I run into the hospital A&E I can hardly breathe. "I'm here to see Erika Williams, she was brought in by ambulance."

The receptionist checks her computer screen. "Can you wait over there please sir? Someone will be out to see you shortly."

I sit down where she tells me to and then I start tapping my foot, waiting for someone to tell me what the fuck is going on. It only takes a couple of minutes for someone to come out, but it feels like forever.

"Sir? Are you waiting to see Erika Williams?"

"Yes I am." I say standing. "Where is she?"

"Are you her husband? Brother?"

"I'm her boyfriend, well fiancé."

"Do you know how to contact her family?"

"Can you just tell me what is going on? Then I can call her family."

"Well you're not really a relative."

"I'm the only one here. I was going to ask her to marry me tonight. We live together. What more do you want to know? How many times a week we have sex? I can give you that information if you want." He is starting to really piss me off.

"That's fine. Come with me and I'll take you to her."

"Finally," I say under my breath, although I guess it was loud enough that he heard me because he turns to face me and then keeps walking.

He stops outside a cubicle and I can hear a lot of commotion behind the curtain. "She's in here." I start to reach for the curtain, but he stops me. "Before you go in Zac, she's in a bad way. We are trying to stop the internal bleeding, but we need to operate. We need you to sign the paperwork."

"What do you mean *she's in a bad way*? I don't care what she looks like. I love her. I just want this nightmare to be over."

He pulls back the curtain and I nearly vomit. My beautiful Erika is laid on the table with her top in ribbons. Her bra has been cut open and everyone can see her tits. Well actually they can't, because there is so much blood on her body that you can't see it's her. She has tubes everywhere. She is hooked up to some machines that are beeping and beeping. There are lots of people in this small cubicle and they're all busy.

I stumble backwards and the doctor is stood behind me.

"Are you okay Zac?"

"What's happening in here?" I manage to say. I feel dizzy and sick.

"We're about to move her into theatre. She has a ruptured spleen, some broken bones, and there is a lot of bleeding, but we can't work out where it is coming from. We need to open her up and see if we can stop the bleeding."

"Do whatever you have to do to save her. Please?" I plead, grabbing almost falling to my knees.

"We will. I promise Zac. The paperwork is ready for you and we will take you to a private room where you can wait. We'll let you know what's happening. You need to ring her family though. They need to know what is going on."

"I'll … I'll do that now."

I watch them wheel her out of the cubicle and I stop them. "Let me talk to her for one minute. Please?"

"Okay, but you need to hurry up. We need to operate immediately."

I stand close to her and touch her face. I don't care about the blood that is on my hands as it is hers. "Baby, I love you. I was going to ask you to marry me tonight." I have to hold back my tears. "You could have just said no. You didn't have to go to these extents to avoid it." I take her hands in between mine and I squeeze them and bring them to my mouth. "When you're better I'm going to ask you again, but Erika will you be my wife?"

I kiss her on the lips and feel my tears drip off my face onto her blood stained one.

"I'm sorry Zac, we really need to go," the doctor says from behind me.

"Bye baby, see you soon," I cry as they wheel her away and into the theatre.

A nurse comes and shows me into the private waiting area and I sit in the chair and sob. I know I have to ring her family, but I can't face it. Picking up my phone I ring the only person I know who can help me.

It rings three times before I hear her voice.

"Mum, I need you." I say before I sob, uncontrollably down the phone.

ZAC is coming on **20th March 2018**.

If you like KEATON and would like to read more, turn the page for a list of my other books. And if you don't want to miss any future releases, please join my http://eepurl.com/djEztr

KRISSY V BOOKLIST

EROTIC ROMANCE

The Lust Train – Newsletter Exclusive Standalone

MIXOLOGY Series

Hunter

Keaton

DARK ROMANCE

My One Regret - Standalone

WHISKEY SOUR Series

Whiskey

Snow

TILL DEATH US DO PART Series

Till Death Us Do Part – Trilogy (For Better or For Worse, In Sickness and In Health, To Love and To Cherish)

To Have or To Hold – Standalone in Till Death Us Do Part Series

For Richer or For Poorer – Standalone in Till Death Us Do Part Series

CHOCOLATE BOX ROMANCE

Beauty Within

0-Love in 6 Minutes

A Taste of Christmas Dublin Style

ROMANTIC COMEDY

Eff This Diet – Standalone

SUSHINE TOUR Series

Sunshine in Madrid

Sunshine at Christmas

Acknowledgments

There are always so many people who need acknowledgements when I write a book. Firstly, my Mum who reads all my books as soon as they are written. I also send her my first, rough, draft and get her opinion on whether I should publish or not. Thankfully, she loves the Mixology Series. Natasha, my PA, also gets my rough copy and tells me if I need to make any changes. Thank you my amazing alpha readers.

One of my biggest supporters for the Mixology Series has to be Samantha Michelle Roberts. She gave me the desire to keep writing this series. I helped her out of her book funk by giving her Ainsley (Book 4 in Mixology Series) to read and she is a big fan of the James family. Thanks Samantha.

Jennifer Foster has been a fantastic support to me. We have become closer and life wouldn't be the same without her in it. She is an amazing friend, pamper and helps me to organise my life. Thanks babe.

As always my readers are so important to me and I

thank each and every one of you for reading my books and enjoying them so much.

Love you lots like jelly tots
Krissy V

About the Author

Krissy V is a loving wife and mother of two teenagers. She loves writing stories and gets many ideas coming to her during her 'real job' in a pharmacy.

Sometimes all it takes is one word and she has to jot down some notes so that she can plot a story.

The Mixology series came about from an incident in work, when she was shaking a kids antibiotic, and that had her thinking about the film *Cocktail* and that's where the James family was born.

For more information:
www.krissyvauthor.com
authorkrissyv@gmail.com

Sneak Peak of Whiskey

PROLOGUE

How did I end up here? My body stinks from not having a wash in about two weeks. There's never any hot water for the showers and I don't even remember the last time I ate.

I hear the guy on top of me grunt as he finally has his orgasm. Thank god! There are only so many times I can count the ceiling tiles in this dank, dark and seedy room.

He rolls off me and I quickly get up and run to the bathroom, to wash away all signs of him.

Men only ever think of themselves and they are incredibly selfish when it comes to shagging. They use my body like a vessel to dump their cum into and then they leave. That's the part I love the most ... the moment when they leave. This is what my life has become. I don't think back to better times when I felt safe, when I felt loved.

I open the door from the bathroom and see Barry on the bed, looking down at his hands. He does this every time, and I know what's coming next. *The guilt trip!* For him not me that's for sure.

He looks up when he hears me approaching. "I'm so sorry Whiskey, I shouldn't keep doing this. My wife would leave me if she knew I was having sex with you … Regular sex with you. Why can't I stay away from you? How did you get under my skin?"

I tune out. He says this every week, it's getting really old. "Maybe you should go to your wife then, buy her some flowers or take her out for dinner tonight. Show her how much you love her."

I'm not upset. I'm not jealous, I'd have to have feelings to be jealous. It just seems to make him feel so much better for cheating on his wife when I send him away and tell him how to treat her nice.

"You're such a good girl Whiskey," he says standing up and tightening his belt. "I was lucky when I met you." He walks towards me and I think he is going to hug me, but he stops short of doing just that.

"So, goodbye then Barry" I say, as I do every week.

He smiles and walks towards the door. "Thanks for being a great sport. I appreciate it and I *will* take my wife out tonight."

Watching him grab the door handle I see him turn at the last minute. "Whiskey, I've left your money on the side. Same time next week then?"

I nod. His guilt trip didn't last long. He closes the door and when I have heard him retreating down the corridor, I lay on the bed and sob. I cry for how my life has ended up this way. I cry for everything I've lost … my family … my friends … my hope … but most of all I cry for losing my dignity.

CHAPTER 1
IT ALL STARTED WITH …..

"Get back in here, Polly!" I hear my dad shouting behind me as I run out of the house, down the path and off down the road. Who calls their little girl Polly anyway? I hate my name and it has been the cause of a lot of our arguments over the years.

"Why did you have to call me fucking Polly?" I scream at him, but he can't hear me as the wind carries my angry cries off and up into the sky.

My full name is Polly Penelope Parker! I mean how bad is that. I get teased about my name all the time – 'Pretty Polly', 'Polly lost her perch.' For fucks sake, what were my parents thinking of – not me that's for sure!

It drives me insane. My dad is a sergeant major type too, which makes it all so much worse. He never stops shouting at me. I can never do anything right in his eyes. I just need to get out of the house today, he was screaming at me about my school report. It wasn't that bad, but dad expects perfection and unfortunately, that is not my style.

I dress weirdly because I don't want people to talk to me, I'm quite brainy but I don't make any effort in class. I don't want the teachers to notice me and bring me to the attention of the other students. So basically, I sit at the back of each class only half listening and then I sneak out and sneak into the next class. Sometimes I feel like I am gliding along on the periphery of my existence.

Life is dull, boring and I can't keep doing this. Something will snap and I don't want to think about the aftermath THAT will cause. I keep walking … I don't know where I am going … I just need to get out of here.

Luckily, I had planned for this day. Not knowing when it would come, but wanting to be ready for it, I had stashed my rucksack in a black plastic bin bag, at the end of the garden under the big lavender bush we have. It is so big that thankfully nothing gets wet underneath it. I left my bag there about two months ago. Just … In … Case … As I walk down the street I lean over the wall, grapple around under the bush trying to feel my bag. I lay my hand on it, thankfully, so I pull it out and hoist it on my back. It's not wet, thank god.

I keep walking … I don't know where I am going … I just need to get out of here.

Moving as fast as I can without drawing attention to myself I can't hear Dad calling after me anymore. I'm in the town centre before I know it and, being a Saturday, it's really busy. I lose myself in the crowd. Even if Dad followed me, which I very much doubt he would, then it would be hard to find me amongst the big crowds..

I continue power walking, not wanting to slow my pace … not wanting to get caught. I decide I know where I'm heading ... to the train station ... Destination unknown!

The lights of the station are up ahead and I know I'm nearly home and dry. My heart is racing, both from the exercise and from the excitement of leaving home. When I walk through the entrance I stop to breathe for the first time since I left home. I bend over and rest my hands on my knees and just breathe. I was never good at running at school. Mr. Peters, my PE teacher, would be proud of me I made it here in double quick time.

The station is packed and I go straight up to the ticket office. It takes five minutes before I'm served and during that time my heart is beating so hard I can hear it in my ears. I keep looking around making sure Dad didn't follow me. Already I know he won't think I've come this far from home having never ventured this far from home before so I know he won't look for me here. The consequence of doing so is just too great. He would shout at me and make me cry and these days I think he is only one beat off hitting me.

It's eventually my turn and I step forward. "How can I help you today miss?" The old man behind the counter asks.

"Good," I say looking around me, not hearing what he asked me.

"Are you ok? Do you need help?"

I stutter, "Erm … Erm no I'm fine thanks. What's the next train that leaves this station? When is it leaving and where is it going?"

He looks at me and then down at his screen. To me it feels like he is taking forever to find a train. I start moving from foot to foot, and I realise it looks like I need the toilet or something. My nerves are kicking in now the adrenaline is dissipating.

"Well miss, the next train to leave is going to Kings Cross Station in ten minutes and it's eighteen pounds and fifty-two pence."

I smile, Kings Cross … that's in London. Do I want to go to London? Will I be able to survive London? Well, if I am going to go to anywhere in the country then London is as good a place as any. I can disappear and no one will be able to find me. It might even be the best place to go.

"Perfect, I'll take it," I say as I hunt through my bag looking for my purse.

"Do you want a return ticket?"

"No freaking way, I am never coming back here again." I say adamantly. Smiling I hand over twenty pounds and wait patiently for my ticket and my change.

"There you go love, platform four and you've got six minutes. Enjoy the capital."

Saying thank you I pick up my ticket and put the

change in my pocket, it will come in handy on the four hour train journey. The journey which will be the start of my new life. Away from here, away from HIM.

CHAPTER 2
LIVING THE DREAM
… OR NOT!

It's been six months since I arrived at Kings Cross Station, with only my rucksack to keep me company. My life has changed so much since then. I have a great job in marketing, a fantastic apartment looking over the skyline of London City and a fantastic man that I love!

Do you really believe that bullshit right there? Life doesn't happen like that – well not for me anyway. Life is shit! That's all I can say. I didn't expect to arrive in London and land on my feet, but then again I didn't really have any type of plan when I jumped on the train that day.

As soon as I stepped off the train, I went to a hostel that I had seen advertised in Kings Cross Station Information Centre and asked if they had any room. My luck must have been in as they only had two beds left for the night.

Before I left the train station I had bought some food and as I went to my room I started thinking about my next step. When I walked in I noticed there were eight beds – eight beds! I'm an only child, so I'm not used to sharing my room! I took one of the spare ones and settled in for the rest of the day and night. Bearing in mind that I am only sixteen, well nearly seventeen, and have never been away from home, not even for a sleepover at a friends, I was really scared. My dad never let me go to my friends houses, he wanted to control me in everything I did. I shook my head to get those thoughts out of my mind.

Google was my friend and I started looking for jobs and bedsits.

I had saved money from birthdays and Christmases for years saving nearly one thousand pounds which I had stashed in my rucksack. I don't intend to squander any of it. I was so tired that I fell asleep straight away that first night, but was woken up later in the middle of the night by my 'roommates' coming home at all hours.

I just turned over in the bed and ignored them. I had watched enough movies to make sure my purse was tucked down my pyjama bottoms so no one could steal it from me.

I woke up before everyone else the following morning and I had snuck out of the room. I made sure I booked another night and went off looking for work. I wasn't going to waste another moment – I need to find work to survive.

My innocence lead me to believe that everyone would be looking for people to work for them, cheap labour, but I was so wrong. Approaching about twenty five different places before lunch was tiring and disheartening because not one of them showed any interested. I stopped to have some lunch in a greasy spoon near Kings Cross and was surprised when I heard them moaning about how busy they were and how they needed help.

Not thinking twice I went up to them and offered my services. The guy looked me up and down, told me I was too young and turned back to getting stressed.

When I looked around there were lots of customers and they were all moaning about something. Without thinking about what I was doing I started clearing the tables, wiped them down and took orders from the customers who looked to me like they were going to leave. After that, they couldn't turn me down. I passed my initiation into 'Silver Spoon' a little café down one of the side streets near Kings Cross.

Silver Spoon was like a second home to me, working about thirty hours a week and then I would go home to the hostel at night. It was perfect except for a couple of the other girls in the room were loud, confident and had a drink or drug problem. Obviously, I didn't drink or do drugs, I was just too young for that.

When I had been at Silver Spoon for about six months, I knew that I needed to find somewhere else to live, but the wages I get from them is just too small for most of the apartments for rent.

"Jane! JANE! Are you not listening to me? Table three needs to be cleared." My boss, Dan, shouts across the café.

Shaking my head to clear the thoughts of finding somewhere to live. I smile at him calling me Jane. Yes of course I changed my name, I didn't want anything to lead Dad to find me. However, when they asked me what it was, I couldn't think quick enough to give myself a really cool name. Jane just slipped from my lips. Jane – as in Jane Doe.

"Sorry Dan, just on that now." He works me like a Trojan and pays me like a slave, but he is a really nice guy who would do anything for me. He is always trying to find out more about me. Where I come from, what I am doing in London, but I never give in and tell him. He knows I'm young, but not exactly how young I am. He asks about my family but I always say that I don't have a family anymore.

Today is really busy, so when my shift is over I take a chance and ask him, "Dan, any chance of a few more hours? I could really do with the money, I need to find somewhere safe to live."

"Jane, I'm really sorry, you know I'd do anything to help you, but I can't stretch to any more hours."

"No problem, I'll have to go and find a second job because I really need to get some more money." I say wistfully as I walk over and clear the tables, ready to close up for the day.

Drifting back to the hostel after work, I'm deep in thought. Laying on my bed I start to cry. Was this really the right thing to do? Should I have just put up with my horrendous life back home with dad? At this moment in time, it feels like I should have stayed and put up with his dictatorship because I don't think I'm cut out for this ... for London.

"Are you ok Jane?" I hear someone who is kneeling at the side of my bed. It's Tilda. She was living here before me. She is gorgeous and is out every night in one designer outfit or another. I don't know why she stays here if she can afford those types of dresses.

Rolling over to face her I put a small smile on my face. She is one of the nicer girls that stay in this room, some of them are absolutely awful to me. Tilda has always been nice.

"I just don't know how to keep doing this. Maybe I should have stayed back home, this is really hard."

"What's hard hun? You arrived and almost straight away you got a job, most of us struggled for such a long time to get any work."

"I know, but I need more money. I can't stay here forever."

"You can stay as long as you want Jane, I've been here for two years. I'm saving up my money so that I can move into a fabulous apartment. Staying here helps me to save, because it's cheap, so much cheaper than a bedsit."

"I can't understand why you don't just leave here, you always look so glamorous, that I wonder why you are even here."

"I'll tell you my story another day. Look, what time do you finish work tomorrow? If you want we can meet up and go for a drink and talk. I'd like to spend some tie with you, we're roommates we need to know each other."

I don't want to tell her that I am only seventeen and can't legally drink. It was my birthday two months ago but I didn't tell anyone. Knowing that if I put some make up on then I will get into a pub no trouble, so there is no need to tell her I'm underage.

"I finish at four o'clock tomorrow."

"Great I'll meet you at the Nag's Head in Kings Cross, it's only around the corner from the Silver Spoon, we can have a really good talk then. I'm off to work now so I'll see you tomorrow. Keep smiling Jane, you have a gorgeous smile." She leans over and kisses me on the forehead and then she is gone. Her action makes me tear us. My mum used to kiss my forehead and thinking of her always makes me cry. We had a happy family until the day she died suddenly. Dad was devastated and that's when he started changing. He no longer showed me any emotion. He shut me out the day she died. I lost two parents that day.

Laying on my bed I think about Tilda. It makes me think about her story, where did she come from? I wonder what kind of work does she do to dress like that every night, and I wonder what she wants to talk to me about.

After a full day at work I'm exhausted and fall asleep easily, only to be woken three or four times during the night, as usual, when the rest of the girls come home.

CHAPTER 3
DECISIONS,
DECISIONS, DECISIONS

Work can't finish any quicker for me. I am dying to meet

Tilda and see what she has to offer me. I really need some work and at this stage I will do anything to try and make something of myself.

"Jane, where are you? I know you're not in this café right now. Earth to Jane!" Dan chuckles behind me.

"Sorry Dan, I was miles away."

"It's ok, I thought you might have found yourself a fella or something."

"No chance of that," I laugh. "I don't go anywhere except here and the hostel."

"Really? You should get out more Jane, you're a very pretty girl."

"Thanks," I blush. "I just want to concentrate on work and get enough money to do something with my life."

"You have great drive and enthusiasm Jane. The way you forced my hand at giving you a job, I'm sure you will be able to achieve whatever you set your heart on."

"Thanks Dan." I do something totally uncharacteristic and I go over and hug him. He pauses for a moment before he wraps his arms around me and hugs me back. I start to whimper because this man has shown me more love in the last six months than my dad ever did. I bet he hasn't even bothered to look for me. He probably thinks that I will stroll back into the house one day, well that isn't going to happen!

We awkwardly pull apart. "Don't you ever tell the other staff I hugged you, they don't deserve hugs." He says smiling at me before he walks away.

"Don't worry, the secret of your soft side will be safe with me." I shout after him.

I hear him laugh, a real belly laugh. It's contagious and it puts a smile on my face.

When my shift is over, I say goodbye to Dan and walk over

to the Nag's Head. Tilda is already waiting for me, thank god. I'm worried walking in that they might ask me for ID, but I had nothing to worry about, they didn't even blink an eye at me.

"Hey Jane, come sit down, I got you a drink." She points to a glass with orange liquid in it.

"What's THAT?" I ask picking it up and smelling it.

"Vodka and red bull. It will give you the buzz, loosen you up a little, you always look like you have the whole word on your shoulders."

"Oh, erm, I don't really drink Tilda."

"What? Who in their right mind doesn't drink as a teenager?" She looks at me like she is seeing me for the first time. "How old are you?"

This is it. This is the moment that I have been waiting for. I take a deep breath, "Eighteen. I'll be Nineteen in May." Well my life did start again when I got here six months ago, so that is now my new birthday.

"Ok, good, because I thought for a minute there you were underage." She laughs. I smile and giggle too, but for different reasons.

We talk for about half an hour about what I'm doing in London and what my goals are. She stands and goes to the bar to get another vodka red bull for both of us. I can feel it working already, I feel hot but I can feel the ice cold of the drink running through my veins. My tongue is feeling looser and my body is starting to relax.

"So, I know you are looking for more work and wondered if you would be interested in what I do. We are looking for someone who looks young, but has some savvy about her. I thought of you straight away. You kind of fit that description."

I take a sip and savour the taste in my mouth. She is

watching me, waiting for my reaction. I swallow with a big gulp.

"W ... What is it you do? I know you are always dressed in gorgeous clothes and I can't ever imagine being able to afford them."

She smiles and smooth's her dress down her exquisite body. "It has taken a while to be able to afford these dresses, but you would be able to as well if you decided to work with us."

"OK. Tell me more. I'm intrigued."

She takes a sip of her drink, then a big breath. "I belong to an agency called Kings X Companions."

I put my glass down. "Go on!" I say hanging on to her every word.

"I know it sounds like we are dirty whores, but believe you me, we are far from that. We escort business men to functions. Being based in Kings Cross is great because we can meet them from the train ready to go wherever they want us to."

Not knowing what to say, I take another sip of my drink, letting it flow through my veins and relax me, because all of a sudden I feel very uptight.

She takes a sip of her drink, carefully watching my face, knowing I won't interrupt she carries on. "We meet them wherever we are told to meet them. We always get a description of them, so we know who we are looking for and they have a description of us too. We spend the evening with them, usually we go for dinner or they take us to an event. Most of these men just want some company while in on business. We also accompany businessmen who live in London when they need to go to functions. We become their plus one!"

"So, you get a free dinner and you get paid for keeping them company for a few hours a night?"

"Yes exactly! Most of the men I have met are really good fun and there are some good looking ones too, which always makes it easier."

"Let me get my head around this. You meet guys. You have dinner, dance a little and then you go home. Is that right? Or do you HAVE to have sex with them too?" I blush at the thought of men paying to have sex with Tilda. She's too beautiful for that.

Her head snaps up to look at me. "I'm not a prostitute Jane!" She is getting angry, but one look at my face and she realises that I wasn't calling her one. I was just curious.

"I didn't mean it like that Tilda, I just don't see how a man would pay a lot of money and not expect sex at the end of the night. That's my assumption from living here for the last six months."

She laughs. "Well in the normal run of things, yes men do expect you to sleep with them, but with Kings X Companions, that isn't the case."

"Well if that's the case then I'd be very interested."

"However," she says, "a man 'might' proposition you and it's up to you whether you sleep with him or not. The company doesn't offer it as a service, however, we are allowed to organise that between ourselves."

"But … but doesn't THAT make you a prostitute?"

"NO! We are high class escorts, that's totally different. A prostitute is someone who sells sex on the corner of the street for twenty, thirty or forty pounds."

"So how much do you make for sleeping with some-one?" I'm really confused. I don't think I understand the difference.

"It depends on the guy really. If he wants sex with you then he will make an offer, but we never accept less than one hundred and fifty an hour. If they want anything kinky, and we're happy to do it, then we charge more.

They might negotiate on a 'full night' where you stay over with them. That figure is up to you, but if it is something you are interested in then I'll help you with that."

"I think I need a drink." I say looking down at my, now empty, glass. I stand and walk to the bar, I know she is staring at me, I can feel her eyes boring into my back.

"Can I have a Whiskey please? Straight up and on the rocks." My dad used to order that and I feel like I need one right now. I used to watch him throw the whiskey into himself and then he would change again. This time he would be stronger, angrier and more determined to make my life hell!

The barman pours one for me and I knock it straight back. It burns my throat, but it's the pain I need. "Can I have another one please and also a vodka red bull? Thank you."

He looks at me and I think he is going to ask for ID, my heart is racing and I make a mental note to get some fake ID. He smiles at me then goes off to pour two more drinks. After I have paid for them I take them back over to Tilda and sit down. "You're pale, are you ok Jane?" She asks.

"I'm just trying to get my head around the whole companion business. I was really excited until you got to the sex part."

She laughs. "Don't get hung up on the sex, Jane. If you don't want to have sex with the guy, then you don't have to. Just like if you are on a date with someone. I'm sure you've been out since you've been here, had a guy approach you and you have thought about having sex with him."

I take a quick gulp of my drink, my last sexual encounter didn't go well at all. I had a boyfriend back home and we had 'experimented' and then I met a guy here a couple of months ago on a work night out. I went back to his place and had sex with him, it wasn't good sex and when he was asleep I crept out of his room and went back to the hostel.

"Oh … my … god you're not a virgin are you?" She says sitting forward in her seat so she is closer to me.

"No I am not!" I say taking another sip of my whiskey.

"That's good you had me worried there for a bit. This is no different to going on a date." She continues. "You spend the evening with a mannerly man, who has been fully vetted and he wines and dines you then you can either say goodbye or stay longer and earn more money."

"Well, when you put it like that it's not too bad then. How much do you get for doing the companion part?"

"We usually get seventy five pounds an hour."

I splutter and nearly choke on my drink "WHAT? HOW MUCH?"

"Shh, stop shouting Jane, you don't want everyone to know. You might start at fifty pounds an hour when you start but after a few months, if you are getting recommendations, then you will move up to seventy five pounds an hour."

I sit there with my mouth open, counting on my fingers. "So, on average you work for maybe six hours at seventy five pounds, that's … four hundred and fifty pounds!" I take another sip of my drink! I think I need it.

"Yes that's about it! It's fun, you get to go to so many nice restaurants, party venues and just have fun. Occasionally, you will go with a really boring guy but it's still worth it for the money alone."

"Can I think about it Tilda? I like the idea of the money, but not sure about the sex part of it. Don't get me wrong, I'm not a virgin. I just don't know how I feel about people paying to have sex with me. In my eyes it's still prostitution, but I don't say as much to Tilda.

"Of course you can, but the reason this has cropped up

now is that we have a customer who is in his early twenties, he has his own gaming company. He asked for a younger girl so you would be absolutely perfect. I said to the boss lady, Carla, that I would let her know tomorrow. Is that enough time to think about it Jane?"

"Yeah I suppose." I need the money and it's easy money to be honest, but what if he asks to have sex with me? I just don't know how I feel about that.

"OK, in the meantime let me show you some of the venues I've been to and some photos of the guys I've met just to try and help your decision."

We sit there for another couple of hours, while she shows me, on her phone, all the photos of her dates and the places that they visited. It all looks fabulous, very much what my dreams are made of. Living the high life and getting paid for it.

"Tilda, can I ask you something?" She nods. "Are you sure I would fit in? You are all so beautiful and I'm just a plain Jane!"

"No you're not. You ARE beautiful, you just can't see it yourself."

"Tilda, look at you – you're gorgeous; blonde curly hair, super sexy figure and you dress to impress."

"I didn't start this way Jane, look." She takes her purse out of her bag and shows me a picture of her when she first arrived in London. She looks a bit like me. Nondescript! I gasp.

"Wow, you WERE like me!"

"Yes, I was. Now YOU can be like me. You already know I have a load of dresses which you can borrow. If you decide to do this and want your own dresses then I can take you out and buy you some clothes. You can pay me back when you get enough money, no rush. I'll also organise a make up session so that you can learn how to apply makeup to make the most of your features. Lingerie is really important, Jane, I can help you with that too."

"Really? You would do that for me?" I can feel my eyes filling with tears, she is being so kind and helpful.

"Yes, you look as vulnerable as I was when I first moved here. Someone took me under their wing and I have always been grateful for that."

"Why do you still live in the hostel then Tilda? Surely you have enough money to move out and get somewhere swanky."

"Yeah I do, but I quite like living with you guys. You keep me stable and grounded. It reminds me of where I came from. I think I would be lonely if I lived on my own. Does that sound sad?"

"No, I feel the same way."

We laugh and get another drink. She's not at work today so we go back to the hostel where she lends me a dress and does my make up. I feel like a little girl playing dress up and when I look in the mirror I can feel the tears starting to build up. I never had this with anyone before. Dad wouldn't allow it and Mum died too early, I was only five when she died. Dad didn't know about my boyfriend and it was hard to keep up the secrecy.

I don't have to worry about that now, I have Tilda and I can't believe everything she is doing for me.

"Don't you like it? You look fucking sexy Jane! No plain Jane tonight!"

"I … I … love it! I look so different. What are we going to do tonight?"

"We are going out! We've got our glad rags on and we are going to p-a-r-t-y!" She giggles. "Come on let's go and show this town what having a good time is all about!"

She takes me to a couple of local pubs and then we go to Madame JoJo's in Soho, I've heard a lot about it, but

I've never been there. I've not really been out of the Kings Cross district since I've been in London. I was worried about venturing too far and getting lost to be honest. Madame JoJo's is a dancing club and there are girls on the stage dancing burlesque and it is mesmerising.

I'm having a great night and Tilda is such good company, I really like her. Our dresses and appearance get us in on the VIP list, I can't believe it.

"This is an amazing night, Tilda. Thank you for bringing me and helping me."

"You're welcome Jane, here's to the future."

We clink our glasses and toast to the future. We keep dancing and being hit on by good looking men until we get home at four in the morning and roll into bed.

CHAPTER 4
LIFE CHANGER

Obviously, I took the job. I mean come on, who wouldn't want fancy dresses, high class restaurants and celebrity parties at least three times a week and get paid to do it all!

Exactly!

I stayed working for Dan in the Silver Spoon for as long as I could, but I had to give that up about twelve months later. I couldn't do the late nights and early mornings. I had cut my hours down and then finally handed my notice in and spent my life working for Kings X Companions. When I first started working with them, they told me my name wasn't sexy enough and wanted me to pick a new one! Tilda jumped in and said 'Whiskey', I looked at her and she whispered, "You always drink Whiskey, so why not?" I nodded and so Whiskey was born.

I had quickly moved from new girl to most recommended and, therefore, my hourly rate increased too. I was earning a fortune!

Yes, I slept with some of the men, but not all of them. It didn't feel wrong, because I didn't have sex with the ones who didn't attract me. That's ok isn't it? Like Tilda told me at the start, it's just like going on a night out and having a one night stand, except I get paid for it!

Tilda and I have talked about getting our own place together, but we are still living in the hostel. We have high dreams and want our first place to be spectacular, we don't want to settle for anything mediocre, regardless of how long it takes.

Madame JoJo's had enthralled me when we had gone there. The women there were so sexy and sensual that I knew I wanted to be like them. It was after going on my first job with the young guy Tilda told me about, that I came to the decision that because of my lack of experience I wasn't sensual enough. I felt clumsy and unsexy around him, so after doing some research I found they were holding burlesque lessons at Madame JoJo's. I jumped at the chance to learn some sensual moves which I could use on my dates.

I found my niche in life:- being a companion, dancing and just having fun. Now THIS is living the dream!

There are a few customers who always request me when they are here in London. I look forward to them coming back, it's like meeting an old friend again, only with greater rewards.

Tonight I am meeting a new customer. I always get a thrill when I get given the details and I try to research them if I can. Tilda is watching me get ready to meet Sawyer Callahan, the CEO for the Callahan group of Nightclubs. He has exclusive nightclubs all over the world and he is based out of New York. He is coming to London to scope out possible nightclubs to buy, renovate and recreate his signature style.

He is attending a charity function tonight in London at The Ivy. I've been there a couple of times and I've really enjoyed it. This time though it is in a private function and there will be lots of business people there rather than an intimate dinner for two. It's easier having dinner in a group, especially if my date is boring. I saw some pictures of him and he is really handsome! Like seriously handsome. I'd find it hard to turn down sex with him if he offers.

Tonight I am wearing a new dress which I haven't worn before. It is different shades of turquoise, starting at the bustier with a dark turquoise and flowing all the way down to the floor to a very pale turquoise. It makes me feel like a mermaid and there is a really sexy split up my left leg, stopping at my mid thigh. Stunning, if I do say so myself!

My hair has been curled by Tilda and then she carefully applied my make up. I finish it off with a turquoise choker that I bought especially to go with the dress. "Wow Whiskey, you look amazing! He is not going to know what has hit him when he meets you."

When I look in the mirror, I gasp. The person looking back at me is beautiful. I can't believe I look so good. I hope he is good company, I feel like tonight will be a good night.

I'm quite nervous, as apart from his nightclubs, there is not much information about him.

"Where are you meeting him?" Tilda asks. We always make a note of who we are meeting and where, just in case something goes wrong.

"His train is coming in to Paddington from the airport in about half an hour, so I'm going to meet him there. I have a plaque with his name on it." I show her the professional sign I had made for him.

"Great, do you want me to come with you and hide, or will you be ok?"

"I'll be fine. Anyway, don't you need to be in Piccadilly Circus to meet Drake?" Drake is her customer for the night.

"Yeah I do, but I wanted to help you if you needed it."

I laugh, "Tilda I'm fine, I'll see you tomorrow, hopefully."

She laughs. "Yeah see you tomorrow." We hug and I leave to make my way over to Paddington. It is buzzing at this time of night. I don't think it is possible to go into Kings Cross Station and for it be empty, the hustle and bustle all starts here. I take a taxi to Paddington and it only takes about ten minutes.

After the taxi has dropped me off I check the arrivals board and see that his train is due in about ten minutes. Making my way to the platform I feel a surge of excitement rush through me. I stand at the end waiting for him with my sign.

Even with the long coat I have on, I know that I still stand out. I look too glamorous amongst all the commuters, the business people and the students.

His train pulls in and I get that fluttering feeling in my stomach, I'm excited to meet him. It's always nice to meet someone new, but there is something about his picture that makes me extra excited.

I see him before he sees me. He is gorgeous, his picture doesn't do him any justice whatsoever. I can actually feel myself blush when he looks up at me and smiles.

"Hi. Whiskey isn't it?" He says taking me into a hug. "Thanks for meeting me." He kisses me on both cheeks. I blush. He grabs my arm with one hand and carries his suitcase with the other. Outside he opens the door to a waiting taxi and I climb in, after he climbs in next to me, he leans forward and says to the driver "Hotel Intercontinental on Park Lane please."

"Right sir."

I have never been to the Intercontinental before and I've heard so much about it.

Sawyer turns to face me. He looks at me for a while and says, "You are much prettier than in your picture." He holds out his hand for me to shake.

"So are you." I say smiling at him as I reach out with my hand. Before I have the chance to shake his hand, he pulls it up to his mouth and kisses it, not breaking eye contact with me.

"Do you know where we are going tonight, Whiskey?"

"I believe we are going to The Ivy." His eyes never leave mine. He has me mesmerised.

"I think we are going to get on well. How did you get the name Whiskey?"

"Don't you think I was born with it?" I ask sassily.

He laughs, "Unless your parents were alcoholics then no, I don't think so." I try not to think about life back home, I shake my head trying to get rid of those thoughts.

Taking a deep breath I say, "Buy me a Whiskey later and I'll show you why." I wink at him. He smiles and then he takes my hand and interlocks his fingers with mine. I feel my whole body shake when he squeezes my hand.

I wouldn't normally be demonstrative with any of my customers unless it was in the bedroom, but clearly he feels he needs to have some contact for us to look like a couple or something.

He is quiet on the taxi journey, but he never once lets my fingers go. He leans back and rests his head on the back of the car seat and then he closes his eyes. This gives me a great opportunity to sit and really take a look at him and study him closely. He is a fine specimen of a man. There will be some very lucky lady out there if she gets to have him in her bed every night. I can just hope I get him for tonight. I shiver at the thought of it.

"Are you cold?" He says, surprising me. He turns his head so that he can see me when he opens his amazing blue eyes.

I can't speak. I don't know how I am going to get through tonight, just looking at him makes me weak at the knees.

"I asked you a question. Are you cold?" He sounds upset.

"No, I'm not. I was just thinking about tonight."

He smiles at me and turns his head back to relax against the headrest.

After a couple more minutes the taxi pulls up at the very grand entrance to the Hotel Intercontinental. I can't help staring at the door leading inside, it is beautiful.

Sawyer pays the taxi, then climbs out holding his hand out for me to take to help me out. I take it and step out into the warm night. He doesn't let go of my hand and he almost drags me into the hotel.

At reception, after he checks in he is given a key to one of the penthouse suites. Of course he does. Where else would this gorgeous businessman stay?

"Do you want me to stay down here while you go and freshen up?" I ask not knowing what he wants me to do.

He looks at me as if I am stupid or something. "No, why would I want that? You are here for the night so why would I want you to stay downstairs while I go upstairs. That doesn't make sense."

I suppose he has a point. He takes my hand again and pulls me so that I get in the lift with him, when the doors close he leans against the wall and just stares at me. He's making me feel uncomfortable, he hasn't even let go of my hand.

"Do I have something on my chin?" I ask with real attitude.

He smiles, "No!"

That's it, that's all he is going to give me. He is starting to really piss me off. He doesn't say very much does he?

When the lift opens, he pulls me out and into the suite. We both stop as we walk through the door. "This place never ceases to amaze me with it's beauty," he says closing the door behind me.

"Wow, Sawyer this place is amazing. It's so beautiful." I take a look around the suite. I'd never be able to afford something like this extravagant.

"Yes, yes it is," he says turning to face me. He takes my second hand and looks me in the eye. He is looking at me so intently that I think he is going to kiss me. I don't know how I feel about that. Usually when a customer kisses me, it's when we are in public and need to put on a front for the sake of business, it's never in private, that would be too intimate.

When he breaks eye contact with me I notice his suitcase is already here. I don't know how it arrived so quick, but he takes his suit out of his suit carrier and then goes into the bathroom to change.

I'm torn between having a look around and trying to sneak a peek at Sawyer changing his clothes. I decide that I would look like a stalker if I did that so I have a look out of the window looking at the view down below.

He comes out of the bathroom and I have to do a double take. If I thought he looked handsome in his business clothes, he looks stunning in his tuxedo. I take a deep breath and swallow hard, he is gorgeous.

"Are you ready to go?" He asks looking at my lips. I can't help but look at his, they look so succulent. "Let's go to the bar and have a drink first, it's going to be a long boring night, so we might as well make the most of it." He doesn't wait for my answer, and after grabbing my hand he turns and pulls me along with him to the waiting lift.

When we get to the lobby we go into the bar - The Lobby Lounge. It's beautiful. "What would you like to drink … whiskey?" He smirks.

"Yes, please. Straight on the rocks please." His eyebrow lifts at one side, he thinks I am joking and don't really drink whiskey. Well, if that's the game he wants to play then I am all over that. I have drunk a lot of whiskey since that first one in the Nags Head with Tilda.

He places my drink on the table and I see that he got the same for himself. I lift my glass and raise a toast, "To a great night, Sawyer."

I smile and he raises his and repeats my toast. "To a great night, Whiskey."

I take a sip and I savour every drop of it. We keep our eye contact, not dropping it once.

"So, what do you think you are drinking?" He asks with a smile on his face.

I laugh, he shouldn't play this game with me. "Well, it's fruity and has a slight almond smell to it." I take another sip and close my eyes to try and break down the flavours in my mouth. When I open them he is staring at me, smiling.

"Well, what else can you tell me?" Ooh he's impatient.

"It has a hint of chocolate and orange, so it could be an Isle of Jura, but a distinguished palette would know it's a Chivas Regal." He smiles, watching my lips the whole time. "However, it's not just a normal Chivas, it's an old one." I take another smell and then a sip. "Now is it a twenty one year old one or the twenty five year old bottle, that is the question?"

His eyes leave my mouth and move directly to my eyes. "I'm impressed so far. See if you can pull it out the bag, Whiskey and if you can then I promise to buy you a bottle."

He's putting the pressure on me now. Those bottles sell for nearly two hundred and fifty pounds each.

After another sip I close my eyes. It's very smooth and more refined so I think it is definitely the older one. "I believe this is the Chivas Regal twenty five year old scotch."

He smiles and his eyes sparkle. "I am extremely impressed Whiskey, you do live up to your namesake. What else are you going to impress me with this evening?"

"Oh I don't know, maybe my wit and intelligence." I smile and giggle.

"Well your giggle impresses me already. I think tonight is going to be fun after all. I was worried that it would be boring, but I can see that it's already exceeded my expectations."

I blush, assuming he is meaning me. This man makes me weak at the knees.

"I'm just going to organise a car to take us to The Ivy so we can get this business thing over with and then we might go to a club and check out the competition."

"Sounds like a plan," I say demurely.

He walks over to the bar and talks to the barman, he is there for quite a while and then comes back over with a smile on his face. "Come on then Whiskey, lets go and have some fun."

He holds out his hand to help me up, I take it. I like the connection we have when his skin touches mine. He lets go of my hand to take my arm and he manoeuvres me towards the front door and the waiting limousine. I always get excited when I am given a ride in a limo as it is such a luxury and I makes me feel like a child going to a big girls party.

Once we are both safely in, Sawyer closes the vanity screen and then he turns to me. "You are really beautiful and I want to kiss you. Is that allowed?"

It's a strange question, maybe he hasn't had a 'companion' before. I nod, "Yes it's allowed … most things are allowed." I don't really want to get into the conversation about sex this early in the night, but it might make the night more fun if we both know what is going to happen at the end of the night.

"Hmm most things. I wonder if the things that I have in my mind that I want to do to you are allowed."

Now I know I am blushing. "You'll only find out if you ask me." I say breathing erratically. This discussion got serious really fast.

He smiles and very slowly he leans forwards, his lips getting closer to mine with every millimeter he moves, it seems like he takes an age. Eventually his lips touch mine, very softly and very gently and then the limo stops and the driver comes through the intercom "The Ivy, sir."

Sawyer groans. He looks at me, "This isn't over by a long shot. I've only just begun." He smiles and steps out of the limo, holding his hand out for me to take. When I stand out of the limo he says, "You look beautiful, I am a very lucky man tonight."

"Yes you are!" I say smiling at him. He chuckles and takes my arm and leads me into The Ivy.

We get shown to the function room in The Ivy. I've never been here before I've only ever been down in the restaurant, which is beautiful, but this is amazing. I can't stop looking around and taking it all in. Very art deco and there are so many beautiful women that I start to feel out of my depth.

When we get to our table, Sawyer pulls my chair out "Sit, Whiskey."

I do and he pushes my chair in, ever the gentleman.

The dinner is magnificent and I can't believe how much I have enjoyed myself with Sawyer; he is funny, has a lot to talk about and he is very gentlemanly.

After dinner we move around the room, Sawyer stopping to talk to people. I stand politely and then he puts his hand on my lower back and maneouvres me to the next person he wants to talk to. This happens for about half an hour and I've noticed his hand doesn't leave my back, even when he is standing talking to other businessmen.

I like the feel of it. I can feel the heat coming off his hand and warming me. We walk up to another couple. They all look the same;- older guy, younger woman who is extremely glamorous hanging off his arm. A little bit like us, I think sadly. The woman in front of us, can't keep her eyes off Sawyer, he hands down beats all the men in the room for good looks.

"So, Sawyer," the gentleman says. "Who is this gorgeous lady you are flaunting around tonight?"

Sawyer looks at me and smiles, his hand moves further around my waist and he pulls me in closer. "This is Whiskey, my date for the night." He leans over and kisses me on the cheek. That's when I feel something I have never felt before in my life. I've read about it, but have never experienced it myself. It feels like he's touched my skin with a bare wire charged with enough electricity to make me jump ten foot in the air. He pulls back quickly and I wonder whether he felt it too.

I blush …

He gasps …

He definitely felt something.

'S … sorry, I need to excuse myself," I look at him and say. He nods and removes his hand from my waist.

After turning and walking away I hear the lady say, "She's not your usual type Sawyer."

I only hear part of his reply, "Thought I'd try something different ……"

I walk quickly to the bathrooms, I need some space. What the fuck just happened? Why did his kiss affect me so much? He's a customer … he's a customer … I need to keep repeating it to myself and remember I'm not on a real date. I think I forgot myself for a while.

I apply my lipstick and lean on the sink taking a deep breath when THAT woman comes into the toilet. She sees me and she smiles. Here it comes … I just know she is going to say something bitchy.

"Hi, my name is Sasha," she says holding her hand out to shake mine.

I extend mine and give her a tight gripped shake. "I'm Whiskey," I answer looking her over, replicating what she is doing to me.

"You're very lucky to get Sawyer, he is a real catch. He pays for all the extras as well." She watches my face as she slips in that she knows I am a companion.

"Did you really think no one knows he is paying for you tonight?" She laughs and it is a real whiny, bitchy laugh. "Darling, he always pays. He doesn't date the same woman twice. He must have gone through all the ladies at Mayfair Ladies and he's now moved on. Where is it you work?"

"Who says I work anywhere? Who says he is paying for this date?" I ask haughtily.

She laughs, like really laughs. "I'm sorry honey, but he

always pays, everyone knows you are an escort! Don't let it put you off, you will be inundated with work after tonight. Everyone wants to have the girls that Sawyer has. You will be loaded by the end of the month!" She gives me one last look and then walks out of the bathroom laughing.

Standing there I feel hurt. I don't know why, but I pride myself in not behaving in a way that someone watching me would think that the man beside me is paying for me. I hate the thought of that, even though I do get paid. I take a few deep breaths, put a smile on my face and go out to find Sawyer.

As soon as I walk out the bathroom I feel someone grab my arm and drag me down the corridor. I start to panic, but the feeling of their hand calms me down, I know it's Sawyer. At the end of the corridor is a small doorway and he pulls me through it and pushes me up against the wall.

"Where were you? You've been gone a long time. Sasha came back and joined us a while ago." He's not angry, he's more concerned.

"I went to the bathroom, there's no law against that you know." Sasha's pissed me off and I can't hold back my tongue. I don't know why I am annoyed that he hires escorts all the time, it shouldn't matter to me, but it does.

He looks at me like I've upset him, then he smiles and moves closer to me. "You've got a little bit of fire in your belly, I like that. Did Sasha say something to you in the toilet?"

He reaches out and takes my chin in between his thumb and his index finger. "Tell me what she said?" He's growling at me.

"She didn't say anything," I say, looking down at the floor.

"Look at me when I'm talking to you!" He almost shouts in my face.

I look up into his eyes, I don't want him to see how much I am affected by him right now. "She didn't say anything."

"You're lying to me, Whiskey. I can tell. Let me guess what she said. She told you that I use escorts all the time. Am I right?"

I nod, as well as I can with his hands still on my face.

"Why does that bother you? Why does it bother me that it bothers you?"

"I … I don't know. I know I'm a whore and nothing I ever do will change that, but to have someone call me out and accuse me to my face, that hurts."

"Look at me and not the floor!" I raise my eyes to meet his.

He leans forward and kisses me on the lips, urgently in between saying, "You …. Are … Not … A …Whore!"

I'm stunned that he kissed me like that. "Sawyer, you and I both know that's not true. I am a whore. I let men take me out and then I charge them to sleep with me. That makes me a WHORE!.." I feel like I want to cry. I have never felt like a whore, not until tonight and I don't like the feeling it gives me. I need to have a serious talk with Tilda tonight because I need to know how I can carry on with this job, thinking the way I do.

He stands back and takes a really good look at me. I feel disgusted, like he is looking to see how much of a whore I really am.

"Whiskey," he says taking my two hands in his. "You are a beautiful woman, men want to date you, where is the problem with that?"

"That's not what I mean – you know that."

"So are you going to change? Are you going to give up

your job because of one woman who works in the same industry as you and is jealous because she is with Bill and not me? That's all it is Whiskey, jealousy. Now let's enjoy the rest of the evening. We can get out of here in a while and go to a nice club I want to look at."

"I'm sorry, you don't need some woman having a meltdown. I suppose that's why you never date and always hire someone."

"Exactly, I don't need this shit!" He takes my hand and drags me out of the room and back to the function room. He then puts his arm around my back and guides me around the room, talking to people as we go. Business as normal.

I feel stupid for being sensitive, but she made me realise what I truly am. I see her and Bill approaching Sawyer and I hold my breath.

She smiles at me and then I see her eyes linger on him longer than necessary. He's right, that's all she is – jealous!

"Are you ok Whiskey?" Bill drawls, smiling at me.

"Yes, sorry I got talking in the bathroom."

"Bill, Sasha, we are going to leave, we have another business engagement this evening" Sawyer says, turning to smile at me.

"I'm sure you do," Sasha says under her breath, but loud enough for me to hear.

I feel Sawyer tense beside me, then he turns me to face him and kisses me in front of them. Now when I say kiss, I actually mean he devours me. I can feel it from the tips of my toes all the way to my lips. I am weak at the knees and he feels me crumble and pulls me closer to him.

When he pulls away I feel a big sense of loss and it's only when I look at Sasha I see that she is stood with her mouth open. "Come on babe, let's go. It was nice to see you both again." He says turning me around and putting his arm around me.

As we are walking out of The Ivy he says "Did you see her face?" Then he starts laughing.

"What's so funny? Do you want to share the joke?"

"I took her out for dinner ONCE, I never kissed her the whole night. I don't kiss anyone … EVER!"

"But … but you kissed me earlier."

"I know!" He leaves it at that and gets into a waiting taxi, making sure I get in before him. He doesn't let go of my hand for the whole journey, but he just looks straight ahead the whole way to our next destination.

When we pull over, I see we are at the Velvet Rooms. I know this as they were around the corner till it's lease ran out and the moved into new premises. I'm excited to go in here and have a big smile on my face.

"Come on, let's go inside and party," he says pulling me behind him.

"Yes, sir!" I say saluting with my spare hand.

We manage to jump the queue, he must have connections. He takes me through to the VIP section and then he goes and orders me a drink – a whiskey. I smile at him as I take it.

We clink glasses and take a sip. I turn to look out at the club and he slides up next to me and wraps his arm around the bottom of my back and pulls me close. "I'm so glad I met you tonight."

"Me too," I say before I remember that this isn't a real date.

He kisses me on the cheek and again I feel the electricity shooting through me. He really does do things to my body that drive me insane.

After mingling for an hour he tells me that he wants to go back to the hotel. This is always the part of the evening

I hate. Will he drop me off on the way? Will he invite me back? Will he want me to sleep with him? What about the money?

"Why are you worrying? What is going through your mind right now?"

I look him in the face and know that I will tell him exactly what is going through my mind because Sasha told me he never sees the same escort more than once. So if this is my one and only chance to fuck Sawyer, then I want to take it.

"I was wondering if you are going to fuck me tonight?"

He looks gob smacked! "That's not very nice language for a young woman, Whiskey. But seeing as you asked so nicely, it would be rude of me to say no!"

I feel myself release the breath I was holding. I smile and then look down at my lap. I don't know what to say now.

"Do you want me to fuck you Whiskey? How much do you want me to fuck you?"

Every time he says the word 'fuck' my pussy clenches. This is going to be enjoyable!

"I really want you to fuck me, hard."

His eyes light up, he obviously enjoys it when I talk dirty to him. I put that little bit of information to the back of my mind for use when we are on our own later on.

"Oh believe me, I am definitely going to do that."

The taxi pulls up outside the hotel and after paying he drags me into the hotel. He stops at the bar on the way. It surprises me, I thought he wanted to go straight upstairs. He says something to the barman and then walks me to the lift.

My heart is racing. I don't know what to expect.

We step inside the lift …

The doors close …

He slams me back against the mirrored wall …

He grabs hold of both hands and holds them above my head …

"Don't move … don't make a sound …"

Is he for real? I feel the heat between my legs and I want to squirm and wriggle.

"Whiskey …"

OK, I won't move then.

He leans forward and puts his spare hand on my thigh, just where the split in my dress is. He groans as his hand touches my skin, the spark of electricity igniting his thirst for me. He kisses me and at the same time his hand is moving extremely slowly up my thigh, towards … towards …

The lift pings and he pulls himself away from me and stands behind me as someone gets into the lift. I can feel his hardened cock against my thigh. It feels huge. I feel the heat pool between my legs and I let out a small moan.

He growls …

We are both breathing heavily.

He moves forward slightly and kisses my neck just under my ear and then he whispers "You're so lucky he stepped in here because I was just going to take you here in the lift. I was ready to press the alarm button and just fuck you. Do you feel what you've done to me?" He pushes closer and I can feel how much he wants me.

"Please …" I whisper back.

"Please what?"

"Please fuck me in the lift!"

He moans, then the lift stops and the man gets out. My heart is racing now. I know I asked him to fuck me in the lift, but I actually didn't think there would be an opportunity to. Now I'm scared, no not scared, I'm excited.

When the lift door closes, he turns to face me. He has a grin on his face.

"Hands above your head!" He orders. I comply.

Then he runs his finger all the way up my thigh until it reaches my panties. He pulls them to one side and then he rips them off me. "Easier access." He states as he rolls them into a ball and puts them in his jacket pocket. His finger moves back and he runs it over my lips and my clitoris. "Oh my god, you're so wet!" He says licking his lips. "I want to taste you, but I'm going to wait. I want to be balls deep inside you right now and then I am going to take my time later on."

I groan, his finger feels so good flicking over my clitoris, he then thrusts his finger inside. "So tight!" he says as his other hand reaches inside his jacket and pulls out a condom. He reaches back and presses the alarm button on the lift and it comes to a shuddering stop.

"This won't take long," he says, as he takes his finger out and puts in a second one.

He puts the packet in his mouth and rips it so that he can take the condom out. He reaches down, opens his zip on his trousers and takes his cock out. He then puts the condom on with one hand. I'm impressed.

As soon as he has it on he takes his fingers out of me and replaces them with his cock. He lifts me so that I am straddling his waist and I move my hands to hold on.

"Brace yourself Whiskey. This is going to be hard!" He thrusts his cock inside me in one swift move.

I gasp, he fills me completely. I've never been so full before. It's a perfect fit.

He pushes deeper. "Fuck me hard Sawyer, please!" I can't wait any longer, I need this as much as he does. He starts thrusting, hard. It hurts ... no it doesn't hurt, it feels right.

He uses his finger to rub my clitoris and I can feel the orgasm building. I feel like I am on the verge of exploding and he only just entered me.

I move my hips as my back is resting against the mirror. I can see both of us on all four mirrored walls in the lift. It's strangely erotic, it's like watching a porn movie but being part of it and it turns me on even more.

"You like to watch yourself?"

"Never done it before."

"So much to do!" He says. He pushes deeper and deeper, he rubs faster and faster.

"Sawyer, I can't hold on."

"Nearly there." He is pushing in and out really deep and it is hitting my spot.

A voice comes into the lift. "Is everything ok in there? You pressed the bell. Is the lift stuck?"

"Fuck" he says. He shuffles me over so he can press the button to talk to the operator.

"Of course it's stuck. Why do you think we pressed the alarm?" All the time he is talking he is pumping in and out and getting faster. I think it won't be long before he is going to explode. The operator better be gone soon, because I don't think I'll be able to keep quiet when I cum.

"Sir, we won't be long, I have an engineer on the way to fix it. Are you alone?"

Sawyer looks at me, smiling. "Don't say anything," he whispers.

He thrusts really hard and deep into me. "No, there is a woman here too. We're fine though, no panickers here."

"That's good, stay calm. We won't be long." The line disconnects.

Sawyer looks me in the eye, "He nearly put me off my stroke, but your pussy was clenching too tight for me to forget where I was."

He pushes … I push …

"Sawyer, I really can't hold on any longer." I push down one more time and then I explode around his cock. I've never come so hard before. I can see stars in front of my eyes.

He watches me unfold and can't hold any longer. "Fuck … Whiskey …"

He leans against me resting his forehead against mine after he has spilled all his cum inside me. He is breathing heavy. After a couple of minutes, he pulls his cock out of me and after taking the condom off he puts his cock back in his trousers. He slowly lets me down so that my feet are touching the ground. "Can you stand up?" He asks me as he can see I'm wobbly.

"I'll be fine, just give me a minute." He pulls me close to his body to support me.

"I just have to get the lift moving or we will be really embarrassed when the engineer turns up."

I forgot all about that. He leans past me and presses the button for his floor and the lift begins to move again. When it stops at his floor he takes my hand and pulls me out and down the corridor to his suite.

Click here to read more of Whiskey's story